# Luvin' A Thug

## Latisha Scott

D1532009

# Chapter 1

The voices in Semeya's head grew louder and became intrusive and split her mind into separate factions, which were at war with each other. One side of her brain said *bitch put your clothes back on. This pussy belongs to Jahlil you is tripping. That nigga is good to us, why are you doing this? You can't go through with this you're going to ruin everything. Cage your inner hoe, lock that bitch up, and keep a tight fist around your panties bitch we live with this nigga. You can't be serious! You don't even know this man, you don't know where he's coming from, what he is trying to accomplish or where he's been or who he's sharing his sex with, if he is disease free or infested with herpes, H.I.V. or if he means any of the things that he is saying to you. All you know is that the words that fall from his mouth sounds good and you like the way that you feel around him. That doesn't mean that the grass is greener on the other side, use your head you poor decision making fool. You're already in a relationship with Josh and he was a damn good catch, why would you mess things up with him for this man who you don't really know, what if he is saying and doing all of this until he gets some pussy and then once he gets it, he bounces on you?*

The other half of her brain was on a different type of time and was with the shits. It kept telling her negative things like *girl fuck that bullshit... this nigga Bay is fine as fuck, he got a couple dollars, he's into you, and that dick! Sweet lord, almighty hallelujah! His big ole dick was so good that it could have been bottled up and used as a remedy to treat loneliness, misery, bad break-ups, and a good enough reason to push nuisance-ass, baby daddies out of the picture.* Semeya hadn't sampled any of his stunning love making as of yet. That didn't stop him from constantly offering it to her.

"You gon' let me get this pussy or not?" Bay breathed his minty fresh breath across Semeya's face. She was pretty to him, she looked Keri Hilson except she was thicker with way more booty. He kissed on her lips while pulling at the top part of her panties. He gently eased his fingers inside of them, delicately sliding them slickly down her ample bottom trying to distract her with loving kisses that wetted up every area around her mouth. Semeya closed her eyes and continued kissing his succulent lips enjoying the attention that he showed her Semeya gasped and grabbed hold of his wrist once she felt his finger enter into her honey pot. Bay twirled his finger around like a little kid scooping up the last bit of peanut butter out of the jar.

"Do you really mean what you said or is you just talking up on some pussy?" Semeya was in her feelings heavily influenced by the few straight shots of Hennessy that she downed upon entering the house party, the few lines of coke that she powdered her nose with had loosening up and trying to recapture all of the lost time that she missed out on while sitting up in the house playing wifey to Jahlil. Bay was all over her whispering inside of her ear and saying all of the right words at the right time, touching her body in all of the right places, and to top it off he smelled good. Semeya gushed and smiled noticing that a lustful spirit had entered into Bay 's heart and caused him to lick along her ear gently causing chills to trickle along her nerve endings. She moved her head away from his lips his tongue flicked and tickled her ear. Looking into his almond shaped hazel brown eyes wetted her pussy and slowly seduced her heart while hypnotizing mind his presence was starting to fuck with her better judgment.

Bay was an extremely gorgeous man his skin color was medium brown, blemish free, and he had a full set of straight white teeth that didn't have any gaps, tiny spaces in between them, or any chipped up and broken off teeth in his mouth. He worked out at the gym regularly and as a result his body was huge and he carried it well he was six feet tall and semi lanky. A lot of people said that he looked like the drill rapper Lil Durk especially when he grew his hair out and dyed the end of his dreads red.

Giving into the voice that encouraged sleazy behavior Semeya ran her hand slowly down Bay 's stomach until she felt his hot penis throbbing inside of her hand her eyes widened in disbelief she was surprised. He had already unzipped his pants and shoved his boxers down to his knees. Bay wasn't playing any games he came into the bathroom with every intention to get some buns. Semeya wasn't expecting to feel his naked flesh when she ran her hand along his body she wasn't aware that he was naked and anticipated pleasure. Seizing the moment before she had time to change her mind Bay smiled during the process of reaching around her body and pulling on her ass and bringing her closer to his erection. "Wait a minute Bay ."

"Fuck that shit Meya we good baby." Bay whispered softly inside of her ear then he licked across her neck then he began kissing all over her face attempting to comfort her by distracting her indecision with kisses. He wasn't about to let her not give him any pussy he wanted her for so long. The two of them flirted with each other every time that they saw each other in passing. Other than that there wasn't much they could do she was always unavailable Jahlil had her cooped up inside of the house the player hating ass nigga was always up her ass and cock blocking making it hard for Bay to get at her. The only time that he ever saw her was when she was at her cousin Jazmine's house playing cards. Now that he had her up inside of Jazmine's bathroom where he wanted her and his opportunity was present he was about to get this pussy and nothing short of falling dead from some unforeseen illness that struck rapid and unexpectedly killing him dead where he stood was going to stop him from fucking Semeya's fine ass. He had to.

"Bay ...ooh." Semeya's eyes blinked his dick was big, but not too big it didn't hurt her it felt good...a little too good she scooted back along the sink. Bay grabbed her ass and pulled her back to him moving forward to meet her allowing his dick to crawl deeper into her pussy. "Get a condom." Semeya legs wrapped around Bay 's waist preparing to feel the pressure had in store for her.

"Dick you down...dick you down... dick you down." Kevin Gate's voice sung from Semeya's phone snapping her out of her temporary trance. She pushed against Bay 's chest. He had to get the hell up off of her she had to answer her phone. Jahlil was calling. Semeya climbed down off of the sink and picked her phone up.

"Hello." Semeya tried to steady her voice she didn't want to arouse his suspicion and make him get on shit.

"Bitch where the fuck is you at?" Jahlil yelled into his phone aggressively. Semeya quickly determined that he was mad based off of the energy that poured into her ear.

"Stop." Semeya mouthed the words seriously while looking at Bay with piercing eyes. "I'm at Jazmine's house."

"Bitch I'm at Jazmine's house where the fuck is you at?" Jahlil frowned he hated wasting his time he wanted everyone who he dealt with moving to his drum and operating on his time anything else pointless he was the man he had all the money and connections. He disliked waiting on people.

"Are you outside?" Semeya was trying to pull her pants up. She was having a hard time the more she pulled them up Bay held onto them trying to pull them down. He didn't care that she was in a state of distressed and overran with panic.

"Talk on the phone." Bay whispered while holding his thumb against his ear with his pinky finger against his mouth. "While I get this pussy." He humped his hips demonstrating to her what he was trying to accomplish.

"No I have to go." The look in Semeya's face convinced Bay that the mood was really over he wasn't about to get no pussy. He pulled his pants up disappointedly and threw his hands up in the air before turning away from her. He backed up a few steps and leaned against the wall staring at her while shaking his head. "I'm in the bathroom where are you?"

"I'm walking up the stairs now."

"Here I come." Semeya's eyes flipped around her head she didn't know what to do. She grabbed the door knob.

"When I'm going to see you again?" Bay had her other wrist in his hand whispering to her.

"I'm around we're going to see each other."

"Let me get your number."

"I can't he be in my phone." She looked at Bay with pleading eyes she needed to vacate the area immediately.

"Please let me get that shit." Bay stared at her with his big beautiful eyes which were now filled with sadness the look in his eyes weakened her disposition and made her compassionate to his needs.

"330." Semeya mouthed off a fake number that was supposed to be hers her number quickly then she opened the bathroom door she damn near fainted when the door swung open and Jahlil stood right in front of her face with the meanest frown on his grill.

"Fuck is you doing?" He looked at Semeya who responded with ease.

"Using the bathroom."

"Who in here?" Semeya looked at him feeling ashamed. Jahlil cut the bathroom light on and walked into the bathroom brushing pass Semeya.

"Why would somebody be in the bathroom with me?" She turned around relieved to see that Bay wasn't standing behind her. He had gotten inside of bathtub and concealed himself with the shower curtains.

"You know how much I hate waiting on mother fuckers...so stupid." Jahlil walked pass Semeya and walked out of the bathroom. "Bring your ass on." Jahlil mumbled under his breath. Semeya looked back in disbelief eventually her disbelief transformed into appreciation. She was grateful that Bay didn't blow up her spot.

## Chapter 2

Jahlil was that nigga as far paper was concerned. He had long term paper. He came from a long line of get money hustlers his granddaddy was none other than Butchie Harris a drug running robber baron who valued capitalism over humanity. He didn't give two shits about people who weren't united in the process of making him some money. He the heart to do what many other wouldn't, the vision to see what others couldn't, and as a result he made millions. Jahlil's father was Michael Harris another hard core street hustling gangster who was meaner than a mother fucker he loved the hell out of some money, but coming in at a close second was his insatiable thirst for bloodshed. People didn't fuck with Michael Harris some say in his younger years people crossed the street getting out of his way when he walked up the sidewalk. Jalil had an older brother Danny Harris. Danny wasn't anything like his father or grandfather people fucked over Danny regularly and if wasn't for Michael Harris making phone calls inquiring about his son's money Danny wouldn't have gotten paid. Danny was flashier than all of them until Jahlil came along. Jahlil was everything that his forefathers were before him.

Jahlil was six four slim built light skin with long jet black hair that he wore it in two long braids that ran along his head and came down pass his shoulders where they hung near his chest. He wore an indecent amount of jewelry he had two Cuban links around his neck one was smaller than the other. He wore nothing less than designer clothes. He had a chipped up Rolex watch that cost a staggering one hundred thousand dollars. Jahlil was a good looking guy with a bushy beard that was groomed so good that it had a wavy appearance. He had houses, cars, guns, and so many niggas around at all times. No matter wherever he went in the world he was heavily protected. He had two twin cousins Amir and Takier those two were stone cold killers who did any and everything that Jahlil instructed.

\*\*\*

Jahlil met Semeya one day while hanging out in the hood chilling with his homies. He sat in his convertible Benz with the top down blasting his music. He pointed his finger in the air while rocking around in the front seat of his car nodding his head around wilding out while rapping the words I'm a hustler and shooter that's a fact nigga. Semeya walked pass the car that he was sitting in on her way to her cousin Jazimine's house when she caught Jahlil's attention. The two of them locked eyes for a brief moment Semeya looked away breaking the connection, however Jahlil couldn't take his eyes off of her he maintained his stare because he couldn't take his eyes off of her she was that fine. Semeya wasn't sure why she continued to looking back at Jahlil. Once she walked up onto Jazimine's porch she looked back again that was all it took the hunt was officially on. She walked inside of Jazmine's house five minutes later someone was pounding on Jazmine's front door.

Jazmine opened her front door and saw Jahlil standing at her door with Amir and Takier.

"Yo where little baby at that just came up in here with all that booty in her pants?" Jahlil was rough around the edges and didn't think there was anything wrong with his opening line.

"Who...Semeya my cousin." Jazmine was a hood bitch with a big booty three baby daddies and had fucked every nigga on the east side of town. Rumored had it she had some good pussy and the head was off the chain, but anybody stupid enough to wife her up was destined for many days of heartache and misery. Jazmine knew what was up and patted her hand against the side of head that shit was itching Bernice had fucked around and sewn her braids in too tight. "You might not like her she's one of those goody...goody school bitches." Jazmine chewed her bubble gum continuously popping it and blowing bubbles with it.

"You gon' let a nigga in or what?" Jahlil didn't wait for an invitation he stepped pass Jazmine.

"Hell yeah you can come in you're always welcome here." Jazmine turned around watching Jahlil walk through her house.

"Little baby." Jahlil called out while walking through Jazmine's house. He located Semeya in the kitchen looking inside of Jazmine's fridge. Enthusiasm popped up in Jahlil's eyes. He walked up on his dream girl and stood behind her with his right hand over his left hand.

Semeya turned around not expecting to see Jahlil and the two men who stood beside him.

"You just gon' walk pass me like that?" Jahlil stared at her with strength in his eyes. He looked at Semeya with his head slightly tilted he looked sexy and dangerous at the same time.

"What else was I supposed to do?"

"Introduce yourself." Jahlil was arrogant and cocky. Semeya wanted to reject his advances just cause she wanted to let him know that he wasn't anyone special and he needed to know that what he did wasn't the correct way to talk to people. Who did he think he was walking up in somebody's house with two goons with him talking about introduce yourself? Unsure how to answer Semeya took her time thinking of a suitable response in the meantime she stared deeply into

Jahlil's eyes taking a tour of his soul roaming over the experiences and struggles that made him the kind of man who he was. In her life men weren't dependable they were violent and abusive...irresponsible childish and never wanted to be held accountable for their decision making. She compared every man to her absentee father and her step-father. Her daddy was all talk and when it came time to love he wasn't available. Her step-father beat her mother ass regularly that she could have easily filed sparring partner as her occupation on her tax returns.

"Do you hit women?" Semeya waited for his answer.

"I put hands on two bitches in my whole life both situations were unrelated incidents. One stole ten thousand dollars from me. The other one set my brother up to get robbed they had it coming. If you're asking do I run around punching bitches to sleep I'm not that type of nigga."

"What do you think about a man taking care of his woman?"

"You want some money?" A look of disappointment sailed into the center of his eyes. He wanted much more from Semeya. He wanted to get to know her and see what she was like. If she was smart, what thoughts occupied her head majority of the day, what her dreams and aspirations were. He didn't see her as the type of female who would sell her body looking for a come up. If she was a thot waiting to get smashed for some paper there wasn't anything that he could do for her except drop his dick off in her and treat her like the freak ass prostitute that she was.

"I don't sell pussy." Semeya rolled her eyes thinking that Jahlil misread her words and tried to group her into a category of females where she didn't belong.

"I'm not asking for your hand in marriage I'm asking for one night see what's cracking with that ass." Jahlil wasn't new to the game and he understood that people said things that weren't true every day all day trying to run game on someone. It was the way of the world especially in the downtrodden slums of the ghettos everybody was out to get theirs and if you had anything of value then you better damn well be ready to throw down and scrap with all of your strength, wits, and resources to keep what's yours. If not someone else who was stronger, slicker, smarter, and more savage than you was going to take your shit. That was just how it was and no one gave a shit if you didn't understand the mechanics of the hood then you became food. He had to try her by offering her cash for sex to see if she would go for it. If she did then he would have his answer if she put up a fight then he would push a little harder until she gave in if she felt disrespected and walked away he could live with that too. At least he would know how to approach her. No self-respecting hoe would walk away with available money sitting on the table if they sold pussy.

"I have an idea that will make us both happy. You can keep your money and I won't have to hurt my hand smacking an arrogant asshole so if you don't mind I have some other shit to focus on." Semeya rolled her eyes at Jahlil who stood there with a crooked smile on his face. "You can use this time to get out of my face." Semeya smiled politely although fury sweltered in her eyes. She wasn't violent there was something terribly offsetting with the way that he approached her.

"So you're not a hoe?" Jahlil was completely smitten with Semeya's beauty it was abnormal for a woman to be that fine and so oblivious of it. That was what made her that sexier in his eyes it was her unwillingness to exalt herself because she was beautiful. She was down to earth and approachable.

"So you're not retarded?" Semeya was angry as she could get her nostrils flared at the same time her eyes narrowed into slices of outrage she wanted to pop off and set Jahlil's artificial ass straight. Jahlil laughed hysterically he put his fist against his lips and laughed before calming down.

"I tell you what go wash your ass and I'll be back here in one hour to pick you up." Jahlil was something else according to the way that Semeya was assessing him.

"I won't be here." Semeya brushed pass Jahlil roughly allowing him to know that she didn't like anything about him. He was an asshole and she could behave just as ignorantly as he was acting.

"Semeya he's just playing with you." Jazmine called out before watching her cousin charge out of her front door with the wickedest attitude.

## Chapter 3

"Hold on little baby." Jahlil hurried outside after Semeya. He skipped down the steps on the porch. He walked fast as he could after Semeya. "Little baby...Little baby." Jahlil jogged after her once he caught up to her he walked in front of her put his hands up while walking backwards attempting to stop her long enough for him to say what he wanted to say. "Little baby hold up."

"Stop calling me that...that's not my name!" Semeya yelled at him she didn't understand how niggas couldn't accept the world no. Damn what the hell was wrong with niggas?

"Whoa...whoa...whoa...stop...stop...stop      nigga damn let me live." Jahlil wanted time to explain himself to Semeya. She wasn't tolerating his disrespect and walking away from him was her way of letting him know that if other hoes allowed themselves to be degraded that was them, but her shit nigga you needed to have your shit way more together than that.

"What nigga...what?" Semeya was growing impatient and frustrated with Jahlil.

"I apologize that's my bad." Jahlil looked at her with his good-looking. "Dead ass I wasn't on shit I had to see what you was about. I'm saying you're rolling with Jazzy no disrespect to Jazmine she get around though. I can't like...like what the fuck I wanna know more about you."

"There isn't anything special about me I'm a person I have a mother and a father." Semeya was still in her feelings. She walked pass Jahlil and he walked after her until he was beside her.

"What about a brother or a sister?" Jahlil walked alongside of her overlooking her attempts at rejecting him. He reached out to grab her hand.

"Nigga." Semeya pulled her hand away from him. "I have one brother and no sister."

"How do you know Jazimine?" The saying birds of a feather flock together entered into his mind he needed to be sure before allowing himself to feel for Semeya and expose the most vulnerable part of himself that she was worth letting his guard down for.

"She's my cousin...all my life she's been my favorite cousin I'm not like her I don't judge her and I don't participate in conversations where others are dogging her out because they don't agree with the way she lives her life. I love her regardless of her personal choices she's still my family." Semeya continued answering questions unaware that Jahlil was sucking all the anger out of her while replacing those emotions with comfort, easy and soothing communication, and he managed to ease her hand into his after several tries. Either Semeya didn't know that Jahlil had her hand in his or she simply didn't mind him holding her hand. When the conversation ended Semeya was in front of her house standing in her front yard staring disbelievingly at Jahlil. He had walked a full one hour side by side with her listening to her run her mouth about things that were important to her. Jahlil wasn't the type of person who listened to someone talk waiting for his time to speak he only spoke when it was necessary. When he did speak he was dropping knowledge on Semeya. No man had ever talked to her like that or stimulated her mind the way that Jahlil did. A quality rare as that was worth pursuing even if it was only for friendship and conversation. The two of them had gotten to know a great deal about each other on the long walk to her house. Semeya agreed to go out with Jahlil for lunch the next day and that one day turned into three years. Jahlil was a good provider, great listener, and a man who took protecting and feeding his family serious.

Dating Jahlil changed Semeya's life tremendously for one she was no longer broke. Walking was no longer her primary mode of transportation. Jahlil made her quit her job and start a business. He showed her how to run a company that depended on other people to run it while she pursued other endeavors like enjoying life and seeing what the world was really like through her own eyes instead of youtube videos and word of mouth stories that bragged about when they wanted to feel important. The only thing about Semeya's life that remained the same was her relationship with Jazimine. She loved her cousin and nothing would keep her away from her. If Jazmine wasn't as ghetto as she was and afraid to explore the world outside of the life that she knew and perfected in the hood Semeya would have taken her on one of her many expeditions.

Jahlil didn't like Jazmine and he hated the fact that he couldn't keep Semeya away from her. Every time Semeya was on the phone with Jazmine Jahlil would talk loud, act rudely, snatch the phone out of her hand then listen to see if Jazmine had snuck and passed the phone to a guy who was waiting to talk to Semeya. If she went to Jazmine's house he would call her phone with attitudes and looking to get into arguments over the smallest things. He wouldn't let her drive any of her cars over to Jazmine's house claiming that she lived in a bad neighborhood and he didn't want anyone to car jack her. Semeya grew tired of fighting him all the time over the issue which he never let go so she agreed to have him drop her off and pick her up from Jazmine's house she reasoned that she didn't have anything to hide. Jahlil wasn't insecure he just didn't trust Jazmine and thought that she had some type of influential sway over Semeya. Jahlil had a really big dick, but didn't know how to use it. He wasn't a great lover he just knew how to hurt a bitch with his eleven inch monster. He sucked at giving head he couldn't eat pussy his idea of pleasuring a woman was swaying his head side to side like Stevie Wonder sitting at a piano sliding his tongue side to side wildly like he was tearing some pussy up. Then he had this move that he swore was mind blowing to a bitch where he used his teeth to gently nibble on the clit Semeya hated when he did it every time he tried it on her he left her pussy sore for weeks. Semeya hardly ever came during sex with Jahlil he had too much and he was missing all the sensitive spots. He didn't seem to care he thought he was knocking that pussy out. He would get on top of Semeya rather she was lubricated or not he would start plowing in and out of her pussy really fast and hard.

Semeya was sexually frustrated she never cheated on Jahlil she went out and brought sex toys and waited for him to fall asleep then she would be up in the bathroom sitting on the toilet sliding a eight inch black dildo in and out of her pussy working it around until it was slicked up with her juices. One time she was so horny she had the stuck the wall while she was down on all fours rocking her hips and dropping it low while fucking the hell out of the dildo doggy style she had her head down on the floor wiggling her ass around when Jahlil walked into the bathroom and looked down at her. She was on the verge of coming so she couldn't stop no matter how embarrassed she felt or how awkward the situation was she could not stop she had her bottom lip in her mouth going in on that dildo she bucked her ass back as her orgasm exited her body. Semeya looked up at Jahlil with dazed and confused eyes that came from busting a fat nut.

"Little baby a freak huh?" Jahlil sucked his teeth and grabbed his dick. "I got you I know just what to do. Clean that pussy up and come get back in the bed I'm tired baby." He walked out of the bathroom feeling inspired to try out some freakier shit with Semeya.

"No Little baby needed to come." Semeya whispered to herself while rolling her eyes.

# Chapter 4

Semeya woke up the next morning with guilt churning around inside of her stomach. She couldn't believe that she was all up in Jazmine's bathroom considering having sex with Bay . Semeya looked over her shoulder and let out a disappointed sigh Jahlil was gone and hadn't bothered to leave a note, kiss her on the cheek or nothing. Occurrences like this were normal. She had developed a hardened disposition to deal with waking up to an empty bed. Jahlil was always gone he was a businessman who overseen a large scale operation. He had people hustling for him in Detroit, Louisiana, Missouri, New York, Atlanta, Florida, and Ohio. His work kept him away from home six to eight months at a time. Semeya wasn't a fool she was aware that loving a man like Jahlil came with a different set of challenges that ordinary women didn't have to deal with. Her phone rang she rolled over and picked it up.

"Hello."

"What do you got going on we turning up over here later tonight and you should be here." Jazmine sounded tipsy like she had been drinking and smoking weed. Kevin Gates could be heard rapping in the background.

"Shit this nigga done pulled a Houdini and disappeared before I woke up this morning." Semeya complained without sounding whiny she didn't have anyone else to express her feelings to except for Jazmine. Any time that she talked to her mother about Jahlil, his absence, and how it was affecting her. Her mother quickly reminded her how advantageous that it was dealing with a man like Jahlil. Her mother's logic was a man was going to be a man at least with Jahlil he compensated her lovely for looking the other way. It could be worse she could get a man to run the streets exactly the same way that Jahlil did to top it off he very well might possibly be violent and kick off in her ass for having an opinion. Adding insult to injury she would have to work, take care of the house, and pick up extra shifts in order to support the supposed to be grown ass man that was making her life hell.

"So he came over here, got you, took you home, made sure you were he wanted you to be, and then he left once you got settled in?" Jazmine sucked her teeth. "Shit couldn't be me soon as his ass left I would be at my friend house with this ass up in the air twerking this big mother fucking around." Jazmine was the epitome of ratchet. She was a good friend who could be trusted slutty or not she and Semeya hadn't ever bumped heads over a man. Fucking behind family was a definite no...no in Jazmine's eyes.

"It aint that easy you know all he does for me I can't just replace a man like him." Semeya didn't want to sound ungrateful belittling the man who put food on her table and money in her purse. Although she felt the complete opposite of what her mouth spoke. She still wanted to sound respectable when talking about the man who changed her life for the better financially anyway.

"Still trying to be dignified, while acting sanctified, all the while looking stupefied." Jazmine rolled her eyes and flicked her tongue breaking the word stupefied down so that she pronounced it stew-PA-fiedddd...duh. "Wouldn't be a bitch like me I'mma act hoe with it drop it down low with it." Jazmine lifted her butt out of her chair high enough to twerk it around then she sat back down. She put the blunt in her mouth and inhaled it before blowing the smoke out of her nose. Semeya laughed so hard and long that Jazmine joined in laughing along with her although she had the slightest idea what was tickling the hell out of her cousin.

"I'll be there damn you are so stupid girl." Semeya thought for a minute she had to choose her words wisely she didn't want to blow up her own spot. "Is TK going to be there?" Instead asking about Bay  Semeya tried to be slick and asked about his friend TK. Jazmine and TK had a weird sex thingy kind of sexual relationship going on where they slept with each other regularly, but denied having feelings for each other, but got attitudes and reacted jealously whenever the other one was entertaining another person.

"Don't...no...see there what we aint gon' do is play on my intelligence." Jazmine inhaled and shut her eyes allowing her high to increase. "TK tells me everything and by everything I mean everything. So whatever sneaky shit you're thinking about pulling with Bay think again bitch."

"I was gon' tell you." Semeya lied there wasn't anything that she despised is man who ran his mouth telling all of his business. She wasn't a trophy piece, she wasn't the girl who was the topic of discussion inside an all men's locker room, and she damn sure wasn't about to split her legs and bust it open for Bay  if he gossiped like a bitch. "What did TK tell you?"

"Bay  just left here picking TK up taking his unemployed ass to a job fair and I told him to stop by later because we were doing a little something tonight. He was like is Mrs Keri going to be there?" Semi blushed listening to Jazmine explain how Bay referenced her.

"I don't know why people say that I don't look nothing like that woman." Semeya rolled her eyes tired of the comparison. Ever since Keri Hilson released her song turning me on every nigga that tried to holler at her started off his conversation by singing Ms. Keri baby. If it wasn't that it was hey little buster.

"But you do don't trip they could be like yo shawty look like Kodak Black." Jazmine shrugged her shoulders and mumbled to herself. "I'm just saying."

"Bye crazy I'll see you tonight make sure Bay is there before you call me."

"You want to make a grand entrance." Jazmine knew the game and didn't mind helping her cousin get her shine on.

# Chapter 5

Jazmine's house was lit people drank and smoked while music thumbed through the speakers. It didn't take long before somebody was up on their feet thinking that they could sing and dance. Liquor made people want to relive their childhood fantasies. All the would be singers who could have made it in the music industry took the room by storm singing off key and sounding like they smoked one too many cigarettes and when they tried to sing oooooooh it didn't sound sultry and seductive like the artist who sang the song it sounded like someone getting out of bed and pulling a muscle.

Steven was in the middle of floor flipping through Jazmine's playlist he found the song that he wanted and turned it on. Everybody young and old all had the same reaction once Keith Sweat's voice came through the speakers.

"Hey!" Jazmine snapped her fingers and poked her lips out and got funky with as she wiggled her shoulders around with an attitude. This was the kind of music that a person had to feel. If you weren't in your feelings, making stank faces, singing offbeat then you weren't listening to the music right. "You run your through my hair you tell me you love me you love me. You act like everything between us is alright girl." Jazmine had joined in with everyone else who all were singing when she noticed Bay walking through her front door. She smiled before shooting Semeya a quick text letting her know that her moment to shut shit down had just arrived.

"Go head Steven!" Someone shouted out encouraging him to act a bigger fool than he already was. He was drunk semi staggering and opening and closing his hand gripping at as much emotional charge as he needed to sing emotionally from his heart.

"I love you...love you...love you oh yes I do my baby...shooby dooby dooby dooby dooby do." He stopped singing for a whole minute he burped and almost threw up so he had to bite down the urge to spill his stomach. When he finally got himself under control and was able to sing again everyone else had taken over and was singing and were swaying side to side feeling the love that radiated from the speakers he joined back in like he never left in the first place. "Ooooohoooo." Steven sang while flipping his fingers in sync with his words like he was actually sounding like Keith Sweat and killing the song when in reality he was laughable at best. He wasn't he was just into it. Steven wiggled his head around while shutting his eyes. His left eye twitched and trembled along with his lips.

"Sing that shit boy!" The same voice encouraged Steven to sing his heart out. When the next Keith Sweat song came on everybody lost their mind again. There was something about playing Keith Sweat's old shit in a party filled with a mixed crowd and you could almost guarantee that everyone in attendance would forget about everything else that didn't have anything to do with loving somebody and sang along to the music.

***

Semeya wasn't playing any games at all she was dressed to impress although she was only going to her cousin's house to play a few drinking games. She still wanted to make her presence felt. She wanted Bay to think about her for years to come. She was tired of being alone and trapped up inside of the house like she was a princess locked away in the tower waiting on her fair prince to rescue her then there was the possibility that he may never come if that was to ever happen then what? She put a lot of thought into her outfit she didn't want to come off as thirsty and looking for attention. She wanted something sexy and flirty that was capable of letting every other female in Jazmine's house that they weren't on her level. Semeya found a pair of blue and ripped up distressed jeans that clung perfectly to her hips, thighs, and ass. She put on a pair of white heels with a classy white shirt. Took another look at herself before smiling satisfactorily. Semeya was ready to show what she was working with.

## Chapter 6

Jahlil sat shirtless inside of a luxurious condo which he used as a stash house whenever he was in St. Louis Missouri. Jahlil smacked his hand lightly against his baby mother's pale face.

"Amber...baby get up...get up baby...Amber!" Jahlil smacked her face again before semi panicking. "Flint call somebody." He put his ear against her mouth listening for signs of oxygen flowing from her body. There weren't. "Flint get on that mother fucking phone and get some help!" Jahlil yelled out while pointing an aggressive finger at his second in command.

"Jahlil we have one hundred and twenty five kilos of cocaine in the back room I don't think it would be wise to call any fucking police over to this house. You been slapping that bitch in the face for the last twenty minutes and she hasn't responded once she's gone, fuck that the bitch is gone." Flint spoke softly while inhaling a gulf of smoke from his Cuban cigar. "That bitch is dead you can't do nothing about that now we find ourselves in a fucked up space. We can't call the cops and we can't just be in with a dead body. We can wrap that bitch up in that carpet and toss her ass out with the trash and keep it moving or we can do the right thing by her call the police and spark an investigation when they find all of this coke." Flint was Jahlil's cousin on his mother's side. He was a heavyset dark skin man with a big bald head full lips and fleshy cheeks. He was all about a dollar and nothing else nothing else.

"That's my mother fucking baby mother nigga you better watch your mother fucking mouth." Jahlil walked toward Flint with a look of destruction on his face.

"What's his name?" Flint never flinched or become excited nor did he take his eyes off of his cousin.

"Who name nigga?" Jahlil was utterly lost and confused he truly didn't know what the hell Flint was talking about.

"Your son?" Flint has a soft low baritone raspy voice that made every word that came out of his mouth sound smooth.

"How in the fuck do I know what his name is?" Jahlil rubbed his fingers across his nose before pulling out a tiny bottle and tap a few drops of coke onto his hand then he sniffed it right up into his nose.

"How old is he?" Flint knew that Jahlil didn't give a fuck about Amber or her son. Jahlil was a heartless and successful drug trafficker who increased the size of the business and revenue through manipulation and force once he took over for his father he had set up drug opererations in the Missouri, Ohio, Louisiana, Florida, Atlanta, New York, New Jersey, and Alabama. He had women in each state watching out for his best interest being his eyes and ears in town while he was out of town. He fucked the women to create an emotional connection with them so he would be in a good position to control them through mind games, money, and isolation. He didn't care about the women they all served a purpose and once they outlived their purpose they were easily disposed of. Jahlil shrugged his shoulders he didn't know how old the son was that he shared with Amber.

"Fuck that do you know what that bitch can do with her mouth?" A look of regret spread across Jahlil's face. He pointed back toward the floor where Amber's naked body lay on the floor. He never looked back. "She don't cut no corners she get right to work and handled hers where the fuck am I going to find a replacement bitch like that on short notice? What am I spose to do?" Jahlil looked dissatisfied with the way things had turned out.

"Cut corners?" Amir's eyes perked up curiously wondering what did Jahlil mean by she didn't cut any corners when sucking dick.

"She can suck dick for thirty minutes nonstop suction sloppy spit everywhere. Other bitches be playing games these hoes cutting corners trying to suck dick until it get hard enough to fuck...cutting corners niggas." Jahlil frowned then put his hands on top of his head.

"I'm fucked up how would you even address that issue, what would you say to the bitch?" Amir shrugged his shoulders.

"That bitch has a real special set of skills." Jahlil held his hands up in the air. "Magical the bitch know how to stretch my nuts out just right. Jahlil's phone rang he looked to see who was calling him. It was Semeya. "Fuck now I got to deal with this." He looked at Amir. "Roll that bitch up in something and dump her body, damn." Jahlil answered his phone. "Hey baby."

"What you doing?" Semeya was dressed checking herself out in the mirror making sure she was flawlessly put together before walking out the front door. She had on a pair of white stonewashed white stretch denim skinny jeans. A simple white shirt that clung to her body and a pair of black St. Laurent platform sandals on her feet had her feeling sexy. Her hair was always put together. She had her hair wrapped in a bob with blond streaks throughout the top part of her hair.

"What's up what do you want shit is crazy out here talk to me I'm in the middle of something." Jahlil picked up his glass of Hennessy and sipped from it.

"I didn't want shit just letting you know that I'm going over to Jazmine's for a little while to play cards and chill out have a drink or two until you get back."

"I won't be back for a couple of months I'm in St. Louis my man baby mother tried to sneak some drugs into the jail for him her stomach acid burned a hole in the bag and the dope spilled into her system killing she died from an overdose."Jahlil sucked his teeth while he lied. Semeya felt sad listening to Jahlil talk she thought that was a unfortunate way for someone to die.

"Wow."

"Yeah so do what you do and I'll call you back right now I'm all kind of fucked up behind this shit. My man is a good dude I got to be there for him and his family. I'll make this up to you. I love you I got to go."

"I love you too." Semeya hung up the phone feeling unsure how to fell she was conflicted her emotions were playing tricks on her making it hard for her to have compassion for anyone else when she wasn't getting her needs met. Jahlil was roaming the globe rescuing and saving everybody else at the same time he was neglecting her leaving her alone to figure out their problems on her own.

# Chapter 7

Bay stood out front of Jazmine's house talking to a group of five men who all congregated around him listening to him tell them a story about the last time he had to shoot someone. From the moment he saw Semeya's candy apple red Range Rover pull up to the curb across the steet from Jazmine's house an interesting smile eased onto his lips.

"I'm going to get with you dudes in a minute." Bay waited a few seconds allowing the crowd to disburse then he walked smoothly across the street and right up on the driver's side of the truck and pushed the door closed at the same time Semeya was in the process of opening it. "We going somewhere else." Bay stared briefly at Semeya challenging her to disagree with what he wanted. Once there wasn't any resistance he backed away from her door and walked over to the passenger's side door. "Open the door." Bay called out after trying to open the door, but couldn't she hadn't unlocked it. That was her way of letting him know that ultimately she had the final say in how things would end.

"Where do you want to go?" Semeya looked at him unflinchingly she wasn't intimidated by him or his bravado act of superiority she dated one of the most scariest men alive Jahlil was a proven murderer who killed people regularly and without conscious.

"My house?" Bay looked at Semeya who shook her head no. "Hotel?" Semeya shook her head no again. "Want to do it in the backseat?" She looked at him like he had gone too far and was starting to become disrespectful.

'What is wrong with you?" Semeya's anger became visible she stared strongly at Bay ready to lash out at him. He was attacking her and coming for her top and all she did was show interest in his hood rat gutter ass.

"The last time I saw you I had this much dick up inside of you." Bay used his thumb and index finger to insinuate an accurate amount of penis based on eye balling system of looking at his hand how much dick he had inserted into her. "I think we need to pick up from there and get it popping." He clasped his two hands together and then slid them apart before looking at Semeya with communicative eyes that had the words what's good burning in the center of them.

"That night I was drunk I was going through some shit. I wanted to party and luckily for you...you were the one who I ended up with. Things didn't happen. I thought to myself hey he's cute, he seems legit why not, let's see where this goes, but you're not interested in getting to know me you're just trying to smash and disrespectfully I might add." Semeya's mouth was dangerous she had the ability to cut a person deep with her words while staring at them with the most delicately pleasant eyes.

"We not going to fuck?" Disappointment bathed in Bay 's eyes. He sucked his teeth.

"No." Semeya shook her head feistily rubbing it in and making sure he knew that he had fucked up with her and wallow in the fact that he was never ever going to get any of her pussy and she knew her shit was good judging by the way the men in her life behaved over her after she had sexed them all crazy.

"Not even in the future?"

"It's not looking like it." Semeya smiled wickedly at him savoring the moment that she dashed his hopes and dreams to bits. It served him right he shouldn't have been such an arrogant asshole. Who did he think he was asking when they were going to fuck like for real nigga is that how you talk to people?

"So can I get a ride to the store?"

"It depends what do you need from the store?"

"I need some condoms."

"Dude." Semeya was offended evidence of her emotions spotlighted in her face.

"I didn't say I needed them for you I just said needed some." Bay chuckled cutely at Semeya before putting his hand over his face. Damn Meya you can't take a joke you're too sensitive I need blunts and shit damn my nigga." Bay 's looked personally at her allowing her to see that he didn't mean any harm he was being an asshole and aggravating her on purpose.

"I like how you just renamed me." Semeya started her truck up thinking to herself how cute Bay sounded saying Meya. Normally she would object to any mutated form of her name her mother named her Semeya and that's what the world was going to call her...not lil Baby not Mimi...and definitely not no damn Meya well Meya sounded cool as long as no one other than Bay tried to call her that.

***

Just like Semeya suspected Bay was ghetto and niggerish he had her take him to the most stereo typical store in the hood. Large groups of people hung out on the corner in front of the store. Crack heads flagged down cars and ran after them yelling yo I got ten dollars. A few dusty bitches stood around in tight clothes trying to look seductive. Semeya pulled up at the store.

"Hurry up." Semeya looked around surveying the area looking at the hood that she grew up in from a different perspective. Back when she lived there it was home sweet home now that she didn't and had been exposed to a different perspective it was a troubled filled community with hazardous social issues that endangered the lives of those unfortunate enough to live there on a daily basis.

"Niggas scare you?" Bay laughed teasing her while climbing out of her truck. He walked along the sidewalk until he disappeared inside of the store. A few short minutes later Bay walked out of the store laughing with a man the two of them shook hands and Bay walked over to the truck. Soon as he got inside he reached into his pants pockets feeling around for something illegal that he forgot that he had on him. He had already passed his gun off to the guy who he was talking to in the store. Earlier when he exited out of Semeya's truck he noticed the cop pull over across the street from the store and cut his lights off plotting on him. When he walked out of the store he saw the same cop car sitting and waiting for him. "Yo this is a real fucked up first date trust me I'm way better nigga than this. I'm a good nigga I can fuck the shit out and I can treat you right I won't tell your boyfriend I'm tapping that ass I won't let nobody know shit that's strictly between us." Bay spoke quickly while moving and preparing himself for something Semeya just wasn't sure what it was at the moment. 'When I get up out of this truck pull off and go back to Jazmine's I'm gon' see you there don't wait don't hesitate just get the fuck up out of here." Bay stepped out of the car feeling on his pockets pretending that he forgot something in the store. He was in the process of walking into the store when a squad car turned up into the parking lot.

"Get against the wall and get your hands up."

"For what...what's up?" Bay didn't budge or comply with any of the cop's request. The cop grabbed Bay by the arm and tried to manhandle him by turning him around forcefully against his will. Bay snatched his arm away from the cop. Semeya looked in her rearview mirror in time to see another cop car pull up into the parking soon as his car stopped the driver opened the door, hopped out of his car leaving his door wide open, and took off running through the parking lot she looked up again to where Bay and the other cop were and saw that they were no longer there Bay had taken off running when she looked away. Semeya didn't waste any time she started her truck up and backed up out of the parking lot then she pulled off.

By the time Semeya made it back to Jazmine's house the cops were out there breaking up a fight between TK and one of Jazmine's other male suitors. Semeya sighed disappointedly she had gotten dressed up for nothing her night was ruined she wouldn't be getting any dick or using any weed or alcohol to smooth herself out tonight she would be at home, alone by herself, sipping wine until she felt a buzz, then she would be busting it open and twerking her pussy all over her vibrator once again.

## Chapter 8

Bay was at home sitting on the edge of his bed surrounded with a multitude of emotions while looking at his phone staring at Semeya's phone number. He thought long and hard about calling her. He wanted to get in touch with her and apologize for the way things had turned out between them the night before. He wasn't trying to be an asshole to her everything happened so fast and his words got twisted then they came out wrong from there the night went to complete shit. He felt in his heart that he needed to make things right with her, but how? What was he going to say to her, my bad about jumping out of your truck and running, shit got hot real quick and a nigga had to slide, but shit what's up tonight though? That definitely wouldn't work Semeya wasn't one of those kick around bitches who allowed men to stomp both feet into her ass and stick around for me. Curiosity burned up inside of Bay he wanted to know more about her he wanted to spend more time around her. He enjoyed listening to her talk. The sound of her voice was sultry and sexual without being explicit. She had a look in her eyes that he couldn't describe he didn't know the correct words to explain it whatever it was made him want to fuck. Bay couldn't believe how twisted he was why was he putting so much thought into calling Semeya? Regardless of how fine she was, how financially set she was, or how different she was than most of the women he knew she was still a woman so why in the Sam hell was he terrified about calling her? Fuck that he reasoned he was a G and G's wasn't scared of pussy that's how he rationalized the situation and found the courage to call her. The phone rang.

"Hello." A female answered the phone Bay was hesitant the voice on the phone didn't belong to Semeya.

"Is this Meya?" Bay 's voice contained a huge degree of skepticism.

"No it is isn't."

"Is this her phone?"

"No it isn't."

"Are you sure?"

"Why wouldn't I be sure this is my phone and this has been my number for the last three years?"

"Dead ass though I met a girl last night we hung out and things got a little sticky know what I'm saying?" Bay fanned his hand around like the caller could see him. "Is you her cousin telling me this aint her phone because she's mad at me?"

"No I'm not her cousin, this isn't her phone, and I've never heard of the person you're inquiring about." She sounded helpful.

"Damn." Bay mumbled. "Dead ass this aint her number?"

"Do you think she gave you the wrong number?"

"I don't think that she would have given me the wrong number I thought we was better than that."

"If she gave you this number she gave you the wrong number." The caller was truthful and to the point.

"Yo why would she do that?" Bay sounded disappointed.

"I don't know maybe she has a boyfriend, maybe she changed her mind about you I don't know that's something you should ask her when you see her again."

"That's fucked up she gave me the wrong number." Bay sighed and shook his head at the same time that the caller chuckled at his reaction he was taking it pretty hard that someone had given him the wrong number. "My bad I'm sorry for calling your house early in the morning fucking with you."

"It's ok." The caller hung up.

"This bitch gave me the wrong number." Bay wasn't used to rejection and kept a handful of women on standby who never said no for situations like this. Hearing no was a blow to his ego and an extremely violent shock to his personality and self-esteem bitches didn't tell him no. He called Rosslyn a definite go head she never said no even if she was on her period she put her mouth to work. "What you doing?"

"Working I told you that I got a new job." She looked at her GPS making sure she was going in the right direction. "Why you need me?"

"You know I do."

"I can come and get you we'll have to fuck in the car after I do my delivery." Anita was a pretty girl with a healthy self-esteem she just liked fucking with different niggas. She sucked a lot of dick that was her thing she enjoyed doing it and driving niggas crazy she felt empowered listening to men beg her to suck their dicks only a handful of niggas could say that they had actually fucked her. Bay was one she liked fucking Bay he was nasty and he had good dick he knew how to get up inside of her big ass. Bay was her boy whenever she needed him he would come through for in every way possible. She never told Bay her inner thoughts or how she secretly thought that when she grew up and got tired of sucking on different dudes dicks that she and Bay were going to end up married. She knew everything about him ranging from his likes and dislikes down to the way how he tied his sneakers. She loved him on the low and would never vocally admit it the circumstances were all fucked up right now and the timing was off. He was loyal to the streets and she loved what she did, but soon as she got done being a hoe and fell out of love with the texture of a new dick sliding in and out of her mouth she would be ready to make him a good woman.

"I'm gon' be outside." Bay  hung up the phone and got dressed.

*** 

Semeya walked around her house with her phone against her ear listening to Jazmine complain about TK and how childish he was.

"Then he ran down the street yelling she fucking nasty pissed me clean the fuck the off." Jazmine rolled her eyes thinking about TK fighting with Patrick in her kitchen. TK caught an attitude because he claimed that she was fucking Patrick because he lit her cigarette for her. When the police came to the house to break the fight up they didn't arrest anybody they were too busy laughing at TK's stupid ass. He was talking shit and wouldn't stop telling the cop that she was nasty. He started crying and told the cop that he wasn't going out like that. The cop told him to calm down or he was taking him to jail then this fool pulled out two hundred dollars talking about he got bail money. Then the cop was like your bail is going to be more than that and TK gon' say well I need to shut up and leave huh the cop was like you should. TK left and we heard him screaming we get outside and he's running up the street yelling she's nasty that bitch is fucking nasty."

"TK is really crazy." Semeya laughed for a few seconds.

"He's not crazy he's stupid."

"I'm saying why he didn't give you the light to light your own cigarette why was he trying to do it for you?"

"Is he there?" Semeya sounded surprised to learn that TK was there at the house with Jazmine. She was talking about him like he had done the most last night and she was over him when in reality she was in bed lying right next to him.

"He right there he came back after everybody left talking about he need me." Jazmine sucked her teeth looking over at TK sprawled out across her bed. The two of them had something going on neither of them knew what it was. Whatever it was energetic highly emotional and very toxic.

"Jazmine." Semeya laughed again.

"Who is knocking at your door this early in the morning?" Jazmine was ear hustling listening hard as she could to see who was coming to pay Semeya a visit so early in the morning.

"That's door dash I order some breakfast."

"How do you know?" Jazmine wasn't buying it.

"I just read the email it said your dasher is outside. I'll call you right back." Semeya hung up the phone and walked to her front door.

## Chapter 9

Bay stood on Semeya's front porch holding her delivery. According to his logic the cosmos were putting the stars in place and lining everything up and he and Semeya were destined to fuck. He didn't believe in luck, coincidentally happenings, or one thing leading into another. He believed in the simple concept of it is what it is and what's gon' be is gon' be and whatever is meant to happen is going to happen regardless of whoever felt what type of way about it. What were the odds of Anita coming to pick him up during the course of making a delivery to Semeya of all people how do you explain that? Shit like that didn't occur so perfectly in movies this shit was meant to be he was supposed to be digging her out and the universe along with God was on his side they wanted them two to fuck there was no other explanation.

"What are you doing here, where is Alyssa Smith?" Semeya searched around looking for a female dasher who fit the description to the profile that door dash emailed her.

"Why did you give me the wrong number?" Bay invited himself into her house he walked in and sat Semeya's food down.

"You can't come up in here you need to turn around and leave. I live here my man lives here and you're in complete violation right now." Semeya stepped up to bumping into Bay pressing her breast into his chest preventing him from traveling any further into her house. She wasn't about to let him ruin her relationship with Jahlil and the life of luxury that he pampered her with.

"Where is Jahlil I'm about to tell him that we was in the bathroom at Jazmine's house doing it Jahlil!" Bay called out and tried to walk pass Semeya who grabbed him by the arm forcefully and struggled with him using all of her strength to stop him from walking through her house. "Jahlil!" Bay called out again he wasn't trying to blow up her spot he was fronting like he was he already knew that Jahlil wasn't at the house he overheard TK and Jazmine talking about how Jahlil leaves Semeya in the house by herself for months at a time. He was making sure she was alone which he thought that she was or else she wouldn't have allowed him to enter into her in the first place. If no one was in the house not a child or a maid then his assumption were spot on the universe wanted them to fuck and he was about to bust a move. "Jahlil!"

"Shut up." Semeya put her hand over his mouth. "What the hell is wrong with you?"

"You hurt my feelings and you're not trying to give me no pussy you think you can just play with people feelings and get away with it? I'm telling on you Jah this bitch out here fuck-." Semeya covered Bay 's mouth and wrapped her arms around his neck and began tussling with him dragging him down to the floor. Bay reached behind his body reaching for her leg. Semeya twirled around doing her best to prevent Bay from grabbing her by the leg she was able to keep him from latching onto her leg for a brief second it took a few tries before he finally managed to get a grip on her leg.

"You need to get up out of my house." Semeya felt her leg being pulled up from underneath her then she felt her body being hoisted up into the air. Bay rushed backwards until he fell over Semeya's end table the both of them landed on her couch. Bay quickly repositioned his body and then yanked at Semeya until he had her pressed down into the couch with her legs in the air holding her ankles and hands together while he yanked at her pants pulling them down. "What are you doing?" Semeya tried to buck her legs it was useless Bay had overpowered her.

"You're not about to keep playing with me." Bay succeeded at pulling her pants down over her ass and down to the back of her knees.

"If you stop now I won't tell Jahlil about this you're still going to get your ass beat if you go any further than this I'm not responsible for whatever he does to you." Semeya was furious that she couldn't break free of Bay 's hold. She should have never fucked with his lame ass dude in the first place he wasn't nothing like the streets advertised according to Jazmine and everyone else he was an official street nigga. According to the behavior that he was demonstrating wasn't nothing street about this nigga except the ground he walked on.

"So you're going to tell Jahlil on me?" Bay smirked before laughing hard as he could. "I want to be scared." Bay laughed again and couldn't help himself he couldn't stop laughing. Do me a favor and tell him this make sure you tell him that I did all this." Bay stuck his tongue out and licked up her pussy then he got down on his knees while still holding her ankles and hands with his other hand. "And add this in there." He licked up and down on her pussy slowly and deliberately before attacking it with fabulously orchestrated strokes of his tongue that wetted her pussy and sent mischief tingling up her spine. Bay ate her pussy so fantastically fine that she no longer resisted his advances she welcomed his tongue she needed it she hadn't come as a result of a human man since she had been dating Jahlil. All her pleasure came from attaching her dildo against the wall and backing her ass up on it. Semeya felt an orgasm building up inside of her vaginal walls and breathed subtly through her nose all the while Bay never stopped punishing her defenseless pussy as it rested helplessly inside of his mouth increasing in moisture his tongue continuously explored her insides swirling around purposefully. Semeya came so hard that she grunted an undecipherable sound that resembled a congested cough. Bay stood up with a proud and shining face he wiped his mouth clean of her juices. "Make sure you tell Jahlil." He smiled before walking out of her house confident that he would see her again and would she came looking for him it would be on his terms. To ensure his plan would go down the way he predicted he left his trap phone under her couch for a little insurance.

***

Semeya rolled over on the couch in disbelief Bay had appeared at her house posing as a Door Dasher, forced himself onto her, performed oral sex on her until she came harder than she ever did in her life. Happiness and relief washed over her then a relaxing sensation overcame her with a sudden feeling of tiredness. Semeya couldn't help herself she dozed off.

# Chapter 10

Semeya woke up later in the afternoon with her eyes and felt around before picking up a phone that was lodged in between the cushions on her couch.

"This nigga left his phone." Semeya sighed then contemplated throwing it in the garbage thinking he must didn't want it if he left it at her house. How important could it be if he mindlessly left it behind? Then she thought again he might use that as an excuse to come back to the house and she couldn't have that. What if someone seen him and pulled Jahlil's coat and let him know that a man was sneaking to his house and fucking around with his woman? She couldn't' risk it. "Hello." Semeya answered his phone.

"Yo who is this?" Bay  fronted like he didn't know her voice.

"Tssk." Semeya sucked her teeth niggas was corny as hell Bay knew damn well who she was. "Boy."

"Naw for real who is this?" Bay smirked playing his game all the way through.

"So you want to play this game, where were you at early?" Semeya rolled her eyes she wasn't as mad as she was pretending to be she was fronting too.

"Aint no telling I be some of everywhere I could have lost my phone anywhere." Bay talked trying to make small talk.

"You didn't lose it anywhere you lost it here at my house. I don't think you lost it at all I think you put it there because I found it stuck in between my couch cushions. You weren't on my couch so if anything you would have lost it on the floor or under the couch so I believe you put it there." Semeya pulled his card she was tired of playing with him.

"Well I'm about to come get it."

"No the hell you're not I'm bringing it to you where you at?"

"I'm at home I'm not going out today." Bay lied he wanted to get her over to his house so he could start what he finished. At his house he wouldn't have to rush he could take his time and service that pussy right and give her what she needed which was some thug loving he was sure that she wasn't being fucked right.

"When I pull up come outside don't have me waiting all day or else I'll leave it on your front porch."

"You didn't get it off the front porch so put it in my hand."

"I didn't get it out of your hand either remember."

"Just bring your ass in the house I'll be looking out for you when you coming?"

"When I get there and I aint your bitch don't be telling me where to bring my ass to." Semeya had an attitude.

"Yet you're not my bitch yet." Bay sounded sure of himself.

"Ever not ever not ever your bitch." Semeya hung up the phone with a slick grin on her face.

Semeya pulled up in front of Bay 's house she got out of her truck dressed in a casual, but expensive sweater dress with matching heels and walked up to the front door she knocked on the door. She looked around semi impressed she thought that he lived in the hood in some rundown neighborhood in some raggedy ass house with a bunch of niggas hanging around out front. He didn't he lived in a nice quiet neighborhood in a decent size house. Looking at him and the way that he carried himself she didn't expect him to live in the house that she was at home. Before she got excited she pumped her breaks this may very damn well be his mother's or grandmother's house. Semeya knocked on the door respectfully just in case any older people lived in the house with him.

"Come in!" Bay yelled loud as he could. Semeya opened the door and shut it behind her.

"I got your phone she called out." She didn't see him she just spoke her piece.

"You need something to drink?" Bay walked out of his kitchen butt ass naked with a puffy dick he had spent the last twenty minutes pumping it up with a cock pump. He walked casually while drinking a bottle of water.

"You just." Semeya stammered she couldn't find the right words to say what was registering inside of her mind. She continued to look at Bay 's penis and finally she gave up trying to locate the right vocabulary she shook her head and tried to look uninterested in his nakedness. "Just...just like fuck it you're on your for colored girls shit just walk up out of a bitches kitchen butt naked on some shit?"

"For one I live here and I walk naked around my house. For two I don't rape bitches."

"You just hold them down and eat their pussy yeah that's a big difference."

"You wanted it."

"Did I now, was it when I Door Dashed my food you picked up the notion that I wanted you to dress up like the dasher who was delivering my food and then did I make you struggle until you made me lie down while you violated me with your mouth?" Semeya sucked her teeth and rolled her eyes with a straight face. Bay smiled and walked right pass her and over to his front door where he locked it. "What did you do that for?"

"We about to fuck." Bay stood in front of the door with a serious look on his face. "And we're going to keep on fucking until you fall in love with me?" Bay walked up on her slowly giving her time to reject or accept his proposal.

"Boy open up this door and let me out of here." Semeya rolled her eyes and scratched a single finger into her hair.

"You don't mean that you want this don't forget I tasted your come and you know what it tasted like?"

"What?" Semeya prepared to fire off at his ass if he tried to clown her and said some ole other shit.

"Like it had been there for a while begging to come out it couldn't cause your man can't get it out. He got that big dick for nothing don't know how to make a bitch cum and his bust too fast. They been saying that about him since forever. Now me on the other hand I'm about to fuck you right, I'm going to fuck you long and strong. I'm going to get that pussy from the back and then you're going to get up on top of me and ride this dick until its sore with pleasure." Bay walked up on Semeya who didn't budge she remained where she stood staring at him unfazed. He palmed the back of her bare legs slowly sliding his hands up them. He ran his hands smoothly under her sweater dress and palmed her whole entire ass. He looked up into her eyes with shock spread out all over his face. Semeya wasn't wearing any panties.

"I need it bad as you want it." She palmed the sides of his face and planted the wettest and sweetest kiss on his lips.

## Chapter 11

Exposure to good dick was dangerous and left an unsuspecting female clueless, discombobulated, and stuck in her feelings. Semeya had a peaceful and serene aura surrounding her she was genuinely happy and unable to sit still. She needed to get outside and do something with herself. She dialed Jazmine's number instead of Jazmine she received a face time call from Jahlil.

"Lil Baby I got some more fucked up news." Jahlil sighed heavily before inhaling a big blunt hard as he could and ingesting a cloud of smoke. He held it for a few seconds then he breathed smoothly through his nose. He shut his eyes and sucked his teeth. "Shit just keeps getting worse remember I told you my man was girl died trying to smuggle some shit into the jail to see him. When my nigga heard the news about his baby mother he dropped dead right where he stood then his mother been gone his daddy aint around the girl's family won't take the baby because it's a mixed child.

The girl had some racist ass parents who still racist they need to grow up and get off that bullshit."

"What about the child?" Semeya stared at Jahlil's eyes waiting to hear what he had to tell her. She wasn't

"This little mother fucker might have to come live with us." Jahlil eyes became saddened. "This game be fucked up."

"Whatever you want to do I'm down with it too I'm your ride or die bitch." Semeya tooted her lips up being silly she was in a playfully mood Bay had her walking on beams of sunrays. She was sore in areas of her body that she hadn't used in a minute. Normally sex with Jahlil was over before it started so she didn't really have time to enjoy the feeling of a hard dick satisfying her. Inserting her dildo inside of her pussy wasn't the same as having a full grown man lying across her body holding her legs up in the air then turning her body sideways with one of her legs held high in the air so he could get more coochie from her. Her neck hurt from Bay doing her doggy style and pulling her hair and holding her hip at the same time.

"You make this shit too easy for me. I'll call you back later." Jahlil hung up the phone happy that Semeya was trusting and believed everything that he said to her.

Semeya didn't believe one word that Jahlil said to her. Niggas were stupid so damn dumb really stupid and didn't know how to lie for shit. Jahlil was nowhere near a caring and considerate person he could give two fucks about a little kid, a dead homies baby mother, all he cared about was money. If he wanted to take care of the little kid it was because the little boy had to have been his son or something along those lines. Other than that she didn't see Jahlil as the kind of person who would do something like that for anybody. Semeya shook her head wondering when will niggas learn that if you want to lie to your chick when you tell the story you have to tell it in a way where she can see you doing the shit that you are claiming to have done. Your woman knows you better than yourself so when you lie she already knows that you're lying. If she hasn't called you on your bullshit it's because she has something else brewing on the stove. Jahlil was lying and Semeya knew it she didn't know why he was lying or what the specifics were all she knew was that nigga was lying.

She didn't have time to play detective she was in a sexy space and wanted to get outside and be seen. Semeya's phone vibrated she looked at the number and steadied her face a tidal wave of emotions suggested that she was feeling Bay as much as he was feeling her.

"What?" Semeya answered the phone with an attitude for no other reason other than the fact that she could besides she wanted to annoy him for some unexplainable reason it brought her joy knowing that she was getting under his skin.

"Shut the hell up don't talk to me like that." Instantly he became defensive Semeya was on shit and playing him like he was one of those other type of dudes who went for sucker shit like that she had him fucked up that wasn't who he was, bitches didn't walk over him fuck she thought this was? It was either pimp or die where he came from he was about to show her something completely different. "I just wanted to see if you wanted to get something to eat. That's the only reason I called. I thought you was tired of sitting in up the house and wanted to get out for a breath of fresh air, but naw I see you're on some other shit so stay your corny ass in the house then I don't give a fuck.."

Irritation could be detected in his voice. Semeya smiled then straightened her face out to match the mood she was about to delve into.

"First of all I have a kitchen, pots and pans, a stove, and food if I was hungry I would cook something to eat. As far as wanting to get me out of the house did I call you saying I need rescuing nigga come save me or was you at home thinking about me and all of this ass and got in your feelings trying to wife a bitch that's already wifed up by a nigga?" Semeya felt for some reason that she was supposed to talk to a man like Bay  with sass and attitude she talked shit to Jahlil, but not to this degree the way she was going in on Bay  was new to her. She hadn't ever talked to anyone in her life like that. It just seemed that a rude ass ignorant disrespectful gun toting animalistic savage like him would want a woman to talk to him like that she didn't know why she just felt it in her spirit so she did it.

"Your pussy aint even all that and your ass don't jiggle." Bay 's eyes came alive with fury he was speaking aggressively through clenched teeth.

"It got a shake to it don't hate on my hate shake." She snapped back.

"Your ass is mediocre at best and your pussy is jive ass alright I had better sex in a jail cell jerking on my own dick. So don't big yourself up shorty." Bay was a liar from the pit of hell and the truth wasn't in him when he denied the glorious truth that Semeya was the best lover he had ever had in his life hands down.

"Well why are you on my phone?" Semeya didn't believe one word that came out of Bay 's mouth. If her ass wasn't popping why was he sniffing up her ass trying to get a refill on her love making?

"That's a good mother fucking question." Bay banged on her.

"Oooh you hung up on me."Semeya laughed and finished getting dressed she knew exactly what she was going to do today she had it all mapped out she was going to ignore the hell out of Bay . He was in for a rude awakening if he thought that she was about to chase behind him. She wasn't like any of the other females who he dealt with. She wasn't impressed by simple shit.

# Chapter 12

Bay hung up the phone feeling extremely aggravated and slightly infuriated that was one of the reason why he didn't have a special woman in his life. Bitches always did some bullshit once they felt like a nigga was feeling them they got real extra. He wasn't about to play this stupid ass game with Semeya. If she wanted to act stupid well then he knew exactly how to come at her he was going to ignore her and avoid her at all costs. In his anger he overlooked the fact that he and Semeya didn't run in the same circle and avoiding each other wouldn't be a problem at all. The only place where he could see her was at Jazmine's house and he didn't have any reason to go over there.

Bay talked all of that shit about staying away from Semeya, fronted like he couldn't wait to see her so he could shun her proving that he wasn't the one, he didn't tolerate any form of fuckery when it came to women. He was convinced that she had him fucked up because he didn't sweat no bitch he didn't give a fuck how fine she was or how curvy her body was that was skin deep superficial shit that didn't hold any weight was all bullshit the first place he went to was Jazmine's house with the expectation of running into Semeya that way he could accidentally see her without intentionally looking for her if it happened that way technically he wasn't checking for her he was really over Jazmine's house looking for TK so she couldn't say that he was over there waiting for her to pop up so she couldn't say he was sweating her although he really was there to see her, but pretending to be there with a whole different purpose in mind. Catching feelings for a person who rocked your body right drove a person insane and had them thinking and behaving crazily.

"Jazmine what's good you aint see TK.?" Bay entered Jazmine's front door without knocking on it no one did Jazmine's front door was always wide open she didn't believe in locking them her logic was somebody might have to run up in her house to get away from the police or something like that. Bay  walked into the kitchen and spoke to everyone before sitting down. He pulled out his phone and hopped on Facebook busying himself preventing anyone from sparking up a conversation with him.

"His bird ass upstairs TK your cousin is down here!" Jazmine yelled from the kitchen where she sat at the table interacting with three other females who she was selling pills to. She pocketed their money and started gossiping. "Finish telling me bitch what happened between you and Jarod?"

"Oh my God I didn't tell you?" Jenelle shook her head she was outdone with her latest conquest of the male species. Jarod (Day-Day) Spencer was a big black defensive end looking nigga he had a wild afro hairstyle, he was really dark skin, and had thick lips that looked like the one on Olmec statue. His lips were big as fuck period point blank he looked mad all the damn time. He wasn't ugly...ugly...ugly, but he drove a Benz and was speculated to go on to play professional football in the NFL. On top of that he was generous with his money other than that bitches wouldn't have paid him any attention at all. Janelle thought that she had come up on a man with big bucks and all of her financial woes had suddenly come to an end when he approached her at a night club. For a while she was having fun riding around town in his Benz while he whipped around his Jaguar. Everything was cool until one night they were having sex and Day-Day asked for a special request. "He was like stick your finger in my butt." Janelle's eyes widened with surprise and suspicion. What kind of man wanted a finger in his butt? "At first I'm like why would you want something like that, then I'm thinking ok maybe that's how he gets off so I stick a finger in his ass and then he said wiggle it around a little bit you know me I'm like fuck it. I'm wiggling it around that's what he wants that's what he gets. Then he was like put two fingers in there...then it turned into three fingers...finally he's down on all fours with his head resting on the pillow and jerking off and I'm damn near punching my fist into this man's butt hole and he's just lying there smiling like he use to this shit. He wanted me to put three fingers into his ass while squeezing the back of his thick ass neck."

"Niggas be gay as fuck out here." Tamia couldn't believe what she heard never in one million years would she ever assume that Day-Day got down like that.

"Bitch for that money I would have sodomized his ass would of had my hand so far up his ass I would have been able to wipe the inside of his stomach clean." Jazmine rolled her eyes while looking serious.

"ILL Jazmine." Tamia burst out laughing. "Niggas is gay...bitches is nasty." Tamia shook her head it would never be her digging in a nigga ass looking for a check.

## Chapter 13

TK came downstairs mumbling under his breath. "What up cuz." He acknowledged Bay and walked fast as he could into the kitchen. He brushed his tall lanky six two one hundred and sixty five pound body against Jazmine's roughly as he could reminding her that he was mad at her.

"Dang TK you all up on my girl." Tamia pointed out TK's behavior. She looked at Jazmine and communicated with her eyes. Bitch what you done did to him?

"Really TK this how we acting like five year olds?" Jazmine walked over to where he stood looking in the fridge he wasn't hungry he wanted to finish arguing with Jazmine he was in his feelings because he felt that she was still sneaking around with Jermaine a guy who she fucked on the regular, but pretended like she didn't the nigga had her so damn open that she referred to as him as her best friend. TK was snooping through her things secretly trying to see if she was still writing Snoop her ex-boyfriend who happened to shoot a nigga and caught a fifteen year prison sentence for shooting Mookie because they both were sleeping with Jazmine. While searching her closets and shoe boxes he found a Rent a center rental agreement for the sixty inch flat screen t.v. that she had in her living room. What bugged him out and sent him into a jealous rage was when he read her references he was surprised to see Jermaine number on the paper along with his phone number. The first thing that crossed his mind was how did the bitch still know that nigga number she told him that she wasn't fucking with Jermaine and lied about ever sleeping with him. TK called the number and when Jermaine answered the phone he hung up and rushed up inside of her Jazmine's bedroom and woke her up by yanking her by her arm and yelling yeah bitch I got your nasty ass. That was three hours ago TK was still in his feelings and unable to let it go.

"Don't talk to me." He shook his head sadness and disappointment appeared in his face. He shut the fridge and walked away looking like he wanted Jazmine to pay attention to him so he could act shady and reject her advances at making him feel better.

"For real my nigga don't talk to you?" Jazmine was so hood she stood up and walked over to TK and reached out to him with both of her tattoo covered arms. "Really TK don't talk to you?" Jazmine got up in his face and tried to wrap her arms around him. TK shut his eyes and shook his head softly he wasn't going out like that. "TK." Jazmine called his name and he continued to ignore her. "TK...TK...TK." Jazmine smiled and wiped her hand over his mouth.

"Chill don't touch me." TK pulled away from her and walked away Jazmine walked behind him and wrapped her arms around him from behind TK bit down his smile.

"You mad at me TK." Jazmine ran her hands up the front of his stomach playing around with him trying to help him lose his attitude. "TK I'm talking to you."

"Jazmine you lied to me you told me you don't fuck with this nigga then I'm looking through your shit and I see not only do you still fuck with this nigga you using him for references and shit. What the fuck I'm supposed to think? If it was me...if it was me...if it was me..." TK looked at Jazmine like she knew better than to do what she did because she wouldn't tolerate him doing it. "I'd be all type of dirty mother fuckers...get out of your house and all that stupid shit, but when you do it...when you do it I'm jealous yeah alright." TK's bulged outside of his head he sucked his teeth then tried to pull away from Jazmine. He wasn't able to she grabbed onto him and pulled at his shirt bringing him closer to her.

"Wait a minute." Jazmine took TK into the living room where they could be alone so she could talk to him and get him to understand her point of view.

"This bitch is crazy." Bay chuckled then shook his head he was on his phone looking at snapchat watching Semeya ride pass Jazmine's house he looked at her snap and it read ten minutes ago. Then he received a message from Semeya he opened it anticipating confirmation that she wanted to get up later that night instead it was a simple message that said dude stop watching my snaps. He messaged her back you wish I was watching your corny ass snaps. Bay chuckled and stood up. He looked around trying not to make eye contact with either Tamia or Jenell he had already fucked both of them when they were in their prime. Jenell used to be fine with a big fat booty compared to what she used to be she was washed up and he wasn't interested. He didn't rummage through the once upon a time bin looking for ex bad bitches. He had an image to maintain he couldn't be seen with just any ole body. Tamia was super fine in her day, but now she had brown stains on her teeth, saggy jeans where a fat ass used to be, she looked like an old woman who had circled the earth a few decades too many and was in bad shape history and struggle were etched into her face, and she wasn't older than twenty five years old.

"Hey Bay ." Tamia broke the ice by speaking first. She gave him a sexy look like she still had it like that.

"Tamia what's good I aint seen you in the hood you got a boyfriend or some wild shit like that?" Bay made small talk not really caring one way or the other if she had a boyfriend. He was merely wasting time until TK finished talking to Jazmine.

"You know I aint gon' do right...all about my money." She rubbed her fingers together.

"Cousin let's get the fuck out of here." TK came out of the living room like he was still upset it was clear to everyone who seen him whatever he and Jazmine talked about in the living room changed his demeanor.

"Ladies." Bay stood up and walked away and then out of the front door. "TK where you going?" Bay didn't want to leave he wanted to hang out at Jazmine's until Semeya fell through.

"I thought you was taking me to auto zone." TK walked toward Bay 's car.

"Why would I take you to auto zone?"

"I texted you this morning and asked you my car won't start aint that what you're hear for?"

"Nigga I aint get no text from you today."

"So what you here for?" TK sulked and became really sad he held his arms out. "You trying to fuck my bitch cousin?" His eyes widened in paranoia TK felt jealousy brewing in the pit of his stomach.

"You said you don't fuck with her like that...you said you don't like this bitch." Bay teased him toying with his emotions for a few seconds.

"That don't mean try to fuck her." TK pushed Bay in the chest area hard as he could. "What's wrong with you? Get your own bitches. Cousin I will fight you over this bitch." TK turned around to walk away after sucking his teeth and fanning his arm dismissingly at Bay . "Don't come over here no more I don't need niggas like you around me...plotting on my bitch nigga." TK mumbled to himself while walking away.

"TK bring your cry baby ass back over here aint nobody thinking about your bitch. I came to give you a ride nigga I got your text." Bay lied he didn't get a text from TK he hopped in his car just the same as if he did get a text from him. TK turned around smiling feeling relieved that Bay wasn't scheming on Jazmine's ratchet ass although she fucked around with him, had a lot of love for him, she still wouldn't care at all if Bay wanted to slide with her she would smash the homie. "Besides nigga I fucked Semeya the other day." Bay couldn't help it he had to tell somebody he knew TK wouldn't tell anyone except Jazmine and he was sure Semeya already told Jazmine what went down.

"I know that pussy good is that pussy good?" TK slammed the passenger's side door. "That pussy good?" He asked one more time sitting in the passenger's seat.

"That pussy good." Bay confirmed it.

"Damn." TK said softly while reclining his head back sighing gently as he could before putting his hands over his eyes. "I knew that was some good pussy. I wish I would have fucked that bitch." TK shook his head then rubbed his hand over his private part.

"What's wrong with you?" Bay started his car up.

"I knew she liked you I aint know she liked you that liked you."

"What you mean?" Bay looked at him quizzically.

"I heard them talking about you one day."

"Nigga you didn't tell me that." Betrayal entered into Bay's eyes.

"I didn't tell you because I didn't know if I heard what I thought I heard when I heard it."

"So what did you hear?"

"I don't know because I didn't hear it." TK was serious and Bay  was frustrated and neither of them could understand why the other was mad and they were no closer to resolving the issue between them. "I heard them say your name and I didn't think nothing of it. You fucked her though that's pimp shit." TK bawled his fist up attempted to pound Bay  up for successfully bedding Semeya's fine ass.

"That is some pimp shit." Bay  smiled for a minute reaching out to pound TK up then he stopped and frowned. "That aint pimp shit nigga I like that bitch. How do I like another nigga's bitch?" Bay  was confused he was used to sidelining women and parking them when they got too emotionally involved with him. He was the back out king who specialized in curbing bitches now he was fully invested in Semeya after one night of wild much appreciated and badly needed sex and she was the one curbing him. It was a completely new experience for him.

"That pussy good." TK looked absentminded, helpless, and powerless to do anything except feel sprung reminding Bay  that pussy had power.

"She got a man."

"A rich man." TK clapped his hands together. "You got paper...her man got paper,paper...paper." TK said the word paper like it was pronounced Payper as a way of letting Bay know that there was a difference between his kind of money and Jahlil's type of money. TK noticed Bay looking at him strangely with a side eye and quickly changed his tone. "You got paper too cousin I'm just saying you fucked her at least." TK shut up and sat back he didn't want to piss Bay off because he needed to borrow some money from him to pay for his parts at auto zone.

***

Semeya couldn't explain what was happening inside of her body or what part of her brain was sending the signal to her heart and what part of her heart was telling her brain she had to make a good impression on Bay . Instead of making her interaction with him one hundred percent sexual she was making him work for her affection she was delivering all of her strong suits right upfront mixed with her good girl persona which wasn't fake she was really the way she portrayed herself the only difference was she was putting some extra care into making it easily visible.

She pulled up in front Jazmine's house with her music blasting the city girl's song twerk. Semeya left her driver's side door open she jogged up on the porch and opened the door then she walked into the house. "Jazz what you got going on up here?" Semeya walked into the house face lit up with happiness. Jazmine smiled instantly recognize the source of her bliss somebody got a raw dose of that vitamin D!

"Bay just left." That was Jazmine's way of saying bitch I know what you did last night.

"Aint nobody checking for no Bay ." Semeya lied unable to contain her cheerfulness. The mere mention of his name had her heart back flipping inside of her chest. The glee radiating from her was so obvious that Tamia and Janell both threw her filthy looks jealous of the fact that they worked hard as hell vying for Bay 's attention.

"Just say you aint because it's a bunch of bitches who is." Jazmine looked around letting Semeya know that she was making a few new enemies. They felt like

Semeya was stepping on their toes and getting in the way of them running into Bay  although he didn't want either of them Tamia or Janelle.

"What you got planned for tonight I feeling like doing something." Semeya ignored Tamia and Janell her mind wasn't on anything except putting her moves down on Bay . Everything else was irrelevant.

"Trying to put together a couple dollars so I can throw something on the grill let me know what you trying to do I could put together a little shing dig in short notice.

"Do that I'll be back." Semeya turned around and started walking away. "Jazmine tell Bay  to stay of my IG." Semeya said before walking out of the front door.

"Petty." Jazmine laughed and felt even more amuse looking at Tamia and Janelle's face all turned up.

"Don't she fuck with Jahlil?" Tamia asked.

"She does why do you ask?" Jazmine already knew the answer, but insisted on playing devil's advocate.

"Bay  is a far cry from Jahlil." Tamia smirked thinking things must not be all too golden in paradise if she's sneaking around with Bay .

"She aint fucking with Bay  like that he be trying to holler she be dubbing his shit." Jazmine lied with ease she didn't want those two jealous bitches having any ammunition to shoot at her cousin with. "Ya'll coming through tonight?" Jazmine pulled out some money and counted it up. "Ya'll feel like riding to the store with me?" Jazmine stood up on her way to get everything that she needed to set the mood for another one of her exclusive banging ass hood parties.

# Chapter 14

Jazmine was the queen of throwing parties. Anytime she threw a party a bunch of people from everywhere came to her house and had fun she was a great hostess. It never failed she always had some type of theme style party going on. This time wasn't any different she had her backyard looking like a beach in Hawaii. The bitch had real sand in her backyard. There were a few wooden torches that had light bulbs in them instead of actual flames. Jazmine had on a grass dress over her bathing suit. She served drinks in big coconuts and served food along with the alcohol and weed that was in heavy rotation.

Semeya was in attendance dressed to kill or incite jealousy whichever one hurt the most she was there making a statement. Everything she did was classy, elegant, and well beyond the average chick's price range. She looked flawlessly assembled and walked around the party confidently and carefree like the rapper Fabolous was walking behind her holding onto his microphone singing girl you be killing em... you be killing em...girl you be killing em...you be killing em...ooooh. Semeya looked around the party searching for Bay doing her best to remain inconspicuous or appearing to be doing anything other than checking for Bay . She was buzzing she had been drinking and puffing on clouds of powerful purple buds.

"Yo Semeya what's good I see you look good up in here let a nigga holler at you." Monk a brown skin man who had the muscular structure of a Greek God he had naturally wavy hair. He rocked a mouth full of gold fronts he had on enough jewelry to rival Mr. T. He was ugly and looked worse than Hell Rell if he had suffered a life threatening car accident. Upon further inspection Semeya could see that his diamonds were fake and his jewelry wasn't shining the way that it should have been. Normally Semeya would be nice about dismissing niggas. Not tonight she was on some other shit blame it on the alcohol and the weed maybe it had a lot to do with the song that came over the speakers.

"Oochie Wally Wally she do her thang..thang...lames get shot down she do it bang, bang." Semeya put her hands in the air like she was holding onto two pistols and act like she was shooting when said bang, bang.

"You can't come at a real woman like that." Jermaine stepped up quickly putting space between Monk and Semeya before things gotten out of control. Monk was out of line for coming at a chick of Semeya caliber. Although niggas put themselves in tight situations being thirsty and when a chick let them know they didn't stand a chance they got bitter and in their feelings wanting to put hands on the female when in all actuality they should have played their cards differently. "Semeya can I live I aint trying to shoot my shot I'm trying to holler at you some good people shit."

"What's up?" Semeya allowed Jermaine to wrap his arm around her.

"You can't be dissing these niggas so hard like that damn girl. I got to walk you away from this crazy ass nigga."

"He aint looking for this." Semeya wasn't a gangster one thing she knew for a certainty without fail if anyone disrespected her or laid one finger on her harm one strand of hair on top of her beautiful hair Jahlil would dress their whole family up in black and fill the front row of his funeral with their immediate family.

"That's real in the meantime you're here alone and Jahlil isn't anywhere in sight before he gets her and extracts revenge you can get it in the worse way. Shoot niggas down politely." Jermaine walked away from her once he got her a safe distance away from Monk. Jermaine was an average height dark brown Haitian man with wavy hair and a strong accent that drove women crazy. He was slender fly all the time dressed like he was on his way to a music industry party. He was a certified hustler who trapped from sun up to sun down and didn't mind making it rain on a female who was partying with him. His one and only flaw was he like to get his nose dirty. He and Jazmine were best friends they had been fucking since middle school when he first immigrated here from Haiti. They still fucked from time to time while they were in between relationship. Jermaine was married and had a lot of bitches to choose from so he wasn't checking for Jazmine at the moment, but he still had love for her.

"What that pussy ass nigga talking about?" TK appeared by Semeya's side his tone of voice and the level of distain that he had for Jermaine made Semeya laugh spitting her drink out of her mouth.

"TK he is not thinking about Jazmine and she is not thinking about him. If you like Jazmine you need to keep it real with her and let her know that you have these feeling so she can stop playing games. I think she likes you too." Semeya put her straw in her mouth and sipped from her drink to keep from asking TK about Bay . If she didn't have anything to occupy her mouth with she would have blurted out where is Bay at?

"Man she know how I feel she just don't give a fuck. She wants one of those rich ass dope dealing niggas." TK frowned while staring at Jermaine walk around laughing and shaking hands. "I should punch this nigga in his face walking around this mother fucker like he the shit cause he aint from here."

"TK you're going to make me choke." Semeya was really tickled listening to TK threaten to kick

Jermaine's ass just because he showed up at Jazmine's party. Everybody came to one of Jazmine's party's expecting to meet someone new because everybody was there.

"Shiidddd that aint going down." TK took off speed walking toward Jazmine when he saw Jermain walking up on her smiling with his arms extended out. Semeya laughed watching TK hurry over to where Jazmine was and intercept the hug that Jermaine attempted to give her with a handshake and fake smile. Semeya looked up in time to see Monk and another man walking over to her. Semeya rolled her eyes she wasn't in the mood for Monk trying to avenge his injured pride. Semeya reached for her taser and realized that she didn't bring a clutch with her. She was unarmed at the mercy of a drunk, jealous, pissed off nigga who was in his feelings because he couldn't get any pussy. Hopefully she would be able to smooth talk her way out of the situation. Semeya looked up and saw Bay standing with his arms crossed over his chest. He looked angry she smiled and quickly removed it from her face she was under the impression that Bay couldn't handle the pressure of chasing her it was starting to draining him now he was in his feelings.

## Chapter 15

Bay walked alongside Jazmine's house on his way to her backyard where her party was taking place. He knew that Semeya was there he saw her Range Rover parked out front. He was dressed in an oversized crispy black hoodie with turquois and red lettering on it with a pair of jet black denim distressed jeans and a pair of turquois and red Louis Vuitton sneakers. His jewelry sparkled brightly from his neck, wrists, and his braids were freshly done. Bay smelled amazing walking pass every woman that he passed on his way into the backyard. They all spoke to him he spoke back being cordial. He wasn't checking for any other woman his mind and heart was fixated on Semeya.

From the moment Bay walked into the backyard the food smelled delicious, the weed smelled even better, and the women looked thirsty for a come up and the men looked famished and broke like they would be begging for some pussy and a place to live. Once he spotted Semeya she was doing a simple two step that she wasn't doing until she saw him then she got on shit pretending like she didn't see and wasn't expecting to see him. A few seconds later he saw Monk's monkey face ass strutting aggressively over to where Semeya stood. Bay thought that he was stunting and getting his shine on at his expense. Monk owed him fifty five hundred dollars over some business that they did and Monk didn't have all of the money at the time. Bay allowed him to leave owing the remaining balance. Monk never called back and he didn't have the decency to answer his phone when Bay called him. The first thought that crossed Bay 's mind was pull out his <u>blicky</u> and air his bitch ass out. He thought for a second before he realized that there was a backyard full of people and potential witnesses and out of all of those people someone would say something so he dismissed the thought. If he couldn't kill him he could at least beat his ass for playing with him. Bay stood where he was frozen in time contemplating his next move while trying to quiet the rage that was growing hotter by the second.

"Yo Semeya what's with that hot shit you was kicking earlier. That was fucked up I thought we was cool? You coming at me like I'm a lame nigga or something like I don't get money like my gun don't go off what's up what type of nigga do you think I am?" Monk was in his feelings and ready to show out on Semeya he didn't care about Jahlil or his goons at the moment he was on some bullshit and this bitch was about to be checked for disrespecting a real nigga in front of all of those people.

"Look Monk." Semeya was in the process of explaining herself when Bay cut her off.

"You look like the type of nigga that come up short on his pack, get a favor from a nigga, and then duck out on a nigga." Bay walked up on him and stood directly in his face with one of the deadliest looks that Semeya ever did see on his face. "Fuck my money at?" Bay pointed his finger in Monk's face daring him to push his hand away. "Pussy boy where my money at?" Bay didn't get loud he didn't want an audience he wanted Monk and Monk alone to know that he wasn't playing with his ass.

"Bay ...Bay ." Monk backed up a few feet trying to put some space between him and Bay .

"What's good?" Bay 's posture went from confrontational to combative he was seconds away from pulling his gun out and going to work on Monk. He wasn't going to shoot him he was going to pistol whip him so good that he would rather preferred to be shot instead of beaten.

"Bay it aint that serious." All of the fight fled from Monk's face disqualifying his gangster as fraudulent and fake. He was a coward who fought women and people who were weaker than he was and that was gangster so neither was Monk.

"Until you give me my money it's always serious. Until you get me my money when you see me walking down the street you cross to the other side, if you riding on the street and see my car pull over and park until I get off that street. If you in the store and I walk up in that bitch drop everything that you're doing and get up out that mother fucker or else I'm taking it personal. Get my money...you aint got time to party you're delinquent nigga run me my paper." Bay 's eyes trembled as he struggled to control his rage. His hands quivered threatening to react without his consent and reach out for Monk.

"I'm leaving Bay  you're right I can't party until I get your money Bay I'm leaving right now."

"Think I'm playing with you?" Bay  stepped up with fury in his eyes and seconds away from dumbing out and hurting Monk. "Now get up out of here."

"Let's go." Monk tapped his man on the shoulder.

"Naw hold that nigga hand and then switch your bitch ass up out of here." The look in Bay 's eyes let him know that Bay  didn't want to let him walk away he wanted to dead him right there on spot. Monk already knew that Bay  had his strap on him and didn't want those types of problems so he obliged. He grabbed his friend by the hand and walked out of the party switching like the bitch that he was. The entire time Bay  walked alongside him with his eyes twitching he wanted a reason to drop Monk. The opportunity never came Monk followed his orders until he got inside of his car and pulled off.

"You must don't like him?" Semeya was standing beside Bay . The sound of her voice pulled him out of his madness and brought him back to reality.

"Fuck that nigga what were you doing with that nigga anyway?" Bay  turned to face Semeya with the same ignorant ass gangster grill that he just punked the shit out of Monk with.

"I don't really know him other than who he is he tried to holler at me I declined typical nigga shit he got mad and wanted to let me know he was somebody special." Semeya shrugged her shoulders and looked at Bay like what you don't believe me?

"Yo fuck this party we going to my house. I've been playing with your little ass all day." He reached out and took Semeya by the hand pulling her away with him. She followed behind him allowing herself to be led away what was she supposed to do? He just got crazy and bitched up another nigga which turned her all the way on her pussy was wet and her heart pounded rapidly inside of her chest. She was high some good weed slightly buzzing from the alcohol and ready to bust it open and give Bay  all of the pussy that he could handle.

***

Semeya wasn't all the way inside of Bay 's house when she felt his hands reaching down into the front of her pants she stopped him before he entered into her vagina she wasn't sure if his fingers were clean after all he had been partying and possibly packaging up drugs earlier that night she wasn't sure if he washed his hands she just wasn't willing to let him dirty up her kitty kat. "I want a shower she continued to kiss Bay .

"That's what you want?" He scooped her up into his arms, carried her up his stairs, all the while they slipped their tongues in and out of each other's mouth.

Upstairs in the shower Semeya washed her body along with Bay 's she ran her hand smoothly over his semi flaccid penis. He kissed her a final time before stepping out of the shower. He dried his body off and then did the same to Semeya. Once he got her inside of his bedroom he transformed from a delicate sweetheart into an aggressive savage. Bay walked up on her put his arms around her and palmed her ass bringing her closer to his body.

"You've been playing games all day taking a nigga through some changes now get your ass up on this dick." Bay palmed both of her ass cheeks and lifted her up off the ground by her behind.

"Like that?" Semeya didn't waste any time she hopped right on Bay 's erection. He walked her over to the bed with his erection still inside of her where he laid her down and got down on top of her in a missionary position and began pressing his hips forward giving her the same degree of potent love making that blew her mind the first time that she gave herself to him. Bay was a nasty lover and moved his hips nastily around grinding into her insides hard and steady swirling his love tool around touching every area of her vaginal walls while delivering that fire. Semeya enjoyed every single inch of his dick pushing in and out of her. Bay flipped her over onto her stomach and laid the front of his body flat against the back of her body. He kissed on her neck and slid his arms along hers until they were completely outstretched then he locked his fingers in between hers and began moving his pelvis up and down side to side stroking powerfully trying to make her cum hard to the point that her body convulsed and shook violently until it became sensitive to touch due to being overwhelmed with delicious feeling sensations. "Oooh." Semeya chewed on her bottom lip while scratching her toes into the bed she couldn't help it her pleasure eased casually out of her as she groaned softly and lowly attempting to hide how turned on she was. Upon hearing the words slip out of her mouth Bay 's grip on her arms became snugger and he stroked harder until his butt cheeks clenched up and he felt fire shooting up his back from squeezing his muscles too tight. He was trying to break her off something off proper. Semeya couldn't help it her insides juddered while she breathed smoothly through her nose allowing her orgasm to pass through her vagina. Semeya's body jerked, quivered, shivered, and quaked underneath Bay 's. He didn't seem to care that he had put it down he continued stroking diligently deliberately trying to poke a hole in Semeya's soul.

# Chapter 16

Semeya and Bay lie in bed cuddling and recuperating after experiencing hours of mind bending sex. Bay was flat on his back and she rested across his chest looking up into his eyes which contained signs of exhaustion. Semeya wrote her name across his chest with her finger repeatedly listening to his heartbeat rapidly then it slowed down before returning to normal.

"Don't start acting crazy, trying to beat a bitch up, stalking me, trying to let it be known that we fucking around and all of that corny shit." Semeya looked at Bay with playfulness in her eyes he sucked his teeth he was getting tired of Semeya coming for him like he was a sucker.

"What makes you think I want you like that? This could be a smash and dash type of thing."

"Pussy so good make a nigga run off on his wife twice." Semeya put two fingers up in the air she didn't feel as confident as she acted, but he would never know.

Bay laughed for a few seconds before shaking his head. He hated a good pussy bitch who knew she had some glass stored safely in between her legs.

"Keep that same energy when you fall in love and this dick gets to getting too good to you. Don't expect you to pop up over here unannounced slicing on my tires, playing on my phone calling, hanging up, and doing all sorts of crazy bitch shit when you find out I'm running around the city smashing bitches left and right all I ask is that you respect the game." Bay had to let Semeya know that he had shit going on he wasn't a slouch ass nigga bitches fucked with him the long way he didn't know what she was thinking.

"I'm a female, but I'm a thug nigga I aint average I aint going be doing all of that unnecessary shit. Don't be tattooing my name on your body don't be outside my house accusing me of fucking your friends don't try to change me." Semeya was serious she wasn't sure how she was going to pull off maintaining a relationship with Bay while being Jahlil's main honey. It was going to be dangerous and difficult task some would call it scandalous, but those were the same people who denied that being human and living life came with unexplainable complications that challenged personal beliefs and cared little about personal preference. Life came at you, however it saw fit, and didn't care nothing about what you wanted. Bay came into Semeya's life upsetting the artificial order of things she wasn't getting dicked down regularly or showered with affection then one day out of the clear blue sky she ran into this big dick pussy crushing gangster who thought she was the closest thing to perfection she couldn't find it in her heart or head to cut him off the way he made her feel was invaluable.

"I'm a side nigga now?" Bay laughed what she was saying to him was laughable at best how was he going to keep it real with the next man's bitch? How could he ever take her serious if she would cheat on her man then it was a guarantee that she would cheat on him. He wasn't about to fall for this shit bitches lied every day and misspoke leaving out bits and pieces of situations acting like she wasn't the way that it was. He had better sense than that. That was his mind reasoning with logic and telling him in advance what life would be like fucking with a fine ass sneaky broad. His spirit song a different tune it drowned out the conversation that the brain tried to carry on. He held onto Semeya lying beside her nonjudgmentally enjoying her presence basking in her power the beauty of a woman was the greatest sight to gaze upon. Bay knew she had a man not just any man a real dope boy who got long money and called shots. A man capable of making his life very uncomfortable with all of that in mind he wasn't the least bit concerned about his safety. His only interest was the song that played insideo f his heart. *He don't do you like I doooo...ooohh....oooooh.*

"No you're my nigga depending on how things work out and how you treat me." Semeya didn't feel like a hoe falling for Bay she felt deserving and entitled to the feelings that he was inciting within her chest. The butterflies fluttered around inside of her like she was thirteen in middle school crushing on a boy who was equally infatuated with her. She wasn't a cheater and hadn't cheated the entire time that she gave herself to Jahlil she respected him and was forever appreciable to the fact that he had changed her life and made it her business to remain faithful to him while they were in a relationship. Jahlil did everything that he wanted to do. He didn't treat her the way a person treated a woman who they loved he treated her like a well-kept sexy ass concubine who had a good shot of love making attached to her body. She was portable and loyal pussy to him and nothing more. A trophy wife someone that made him look good. He financed a lavish lifestyle for her to compensate for all of the time that she spent alone. Until Bay made a move on her she never paid attention to how lonely and dissatisfied she really felt. She thought that she was happy...how could she not be? She thought she was content with her life she thought Jahlil was a good man and would change when his lifestyle allowed him to slow down. She didn't want to add any pressure or stress into his already stressful life. All of that changed when Bay started pursuing her. The thrill of the chase was so exciting and fun to her that she fronted on him extra hard forcing him to chase her down because she loved the attention. He wanted her so badly that he endured everything that came with her and he wanted more of her time fully aware that she had a man and she could never be anything more to him than a moment to experience. He didn't care he wanted her that badly even if it was only for one night he still had to have her and was willing to go to extreme lengths even risking his life to get her and that made her feel sexier and confident as a woman something she would never admit to him.

"How does that work?" Bay wasn't buying anything that she was saying he knew that good sex encouraged excessive talking that didn't mean anything without action backing it up so he entertained Semeya's rambling and meaningless talk overlooking the fact that the two of them were severely attracted to each other.

"I don't know I've never done this before." Honesty was the rawest of emotions and always got rejected due to its simplistic nature. Something as incredibly influential as the increasing feelings developing between them was too resilient to be summed up by saying I don't know, but that was life. It didn't always make sense it just felt right. From a moral point of view Semeya shouldn't have ever been in Bay 's bed while being in a relationship with Jahlil she was dead ass wrong from a humanistic view the way that Bay made her feel overshadowed common sense, better judgment, and anything anybody had to say about her. When he licked her lips and kissed her pussy heaven became real the way he touched her had her vulnerable and at his mercy. It couldn't be explained outside of the connection between two people experiencing it, but it was very real it was a spiritual agreement between two souls one wanted love and the other wanted to give it.

"I must be retarted as hell because this crazy shit you talking is making sense to me." Bay wrapped Semeya in his arms and kissed her on the forehead. He didn't want to think, he didn't want to put a title on what he had with Semeya all he wanted was to continue to have it.

## Chapter 17

Semeya felt good sitting beside Jazmine on a private jet they were on their way to Miami for the weekend her body was relaxed and exhilarated and had her focused on the fact that she was able to do anything that she set her mind to Right now her mind was concentrating on spending as much time as she could with Bay . It felt good waking up to him there was no way for her to wake up to him every day where they were from someone would see her truck and put two and two together and then their spot would be blown up. She put together a trip on short notice. She paid for the entire trip even paid her aunt Jazmine's mother to keep Jazmine's kids while they got away for the weekend. She paid TK and Bay 's tickets except they couldn't get on the jet with her and Jazmine. They had to get on a plane and meet them in Miami. Semeya rented out a mini mansion for the weekend. She had been to Miami many times before and wasn't pressed about sightseeing and taking in the cultural nightlife of the beautiful and very expensive city of Miami. It was fun and exciting, but spending time alone with Bay was her sole objective and worth every dollar she invested in the trip.

Once the plane landed Semeya and Jazmine walked off the plane and got into a Rolls Royce phantom. Jazmine couldn't believe her eyes looking at the car she had never seen anything as elegant and luxurious as the car in her life.

"Semeya girl." Jazmine looked around the inside of the car in disbelief her mouth hung open in awe she wasn't aware that her cousin was living so good. "I'm mad at you why haven't you been inviting me to come with you?"

"I never thought that you were into this type of stuff." Semeya shrugged her shoulders nonchalantly accustomed to the lifestyle that had Jazmine star struck.

"Bitch." Jazmine called out playfully pronouncing the word in a way that made it sound like beachhhhh. Semeya laughed and shook her head thinking that if

Jazmine was impressed with the jet ride and the car that she was riding in then she would be bugged eyed and gawking over the houses once she saw them.

***

TK was on the airplane scared out of his mind he had never flown before. He was visibly nervous and wasn't able to calm himself down. He chewed vigorously on the piece of gum that Bay had given him.

"TK." Bay called his name teasing him TK was terrified and was trying to remain quiet. Bay wanted to get him talking to ease the tension that had his cousin boxed in.

"Bay what's up why you keep fucking with me?" TK rolled his eyes and leaned his head to the left he was distressed and irritated this wasn't aware that this was the first time Bay had spoken to him.

"You want to use my laptop to watch a movie?" Bay looked at him holding back his smile.

"No." The look on TK's face was priceless he looked like he was suffering from indigestion.

"You got to use the bathroom?" Bay looked across the isles at TK.

"Bay damn." TK said his name like Len...NAY dayum.

"Alright." Bay laughed at him and sat back turning his music up in his ear buds. He looked over at TK who had closed his eyes as the plane began moving. Once the plane ascended into the air Bay watched TK inhale deeply while leaning back in his seat and holding onto his leg. He smiled before chuckling to himself.

Soon as the plane landed Bay and TK were inside of the rental car that Semeya rented for them speeding up the street with the music blasting. TK hadn't been outside of his hometown and it showed when he kept pointing out the window.

"Look at those white bitches." He was like a kid in a candy store looking at all of the different beautiful women. "Aye mamacita!" TK yelled out the window. "My beautiful peacan Ricans." TK was basking in his glory feasting his eyes on so many thick bodied women. "All shit the mother of the universe look at all of my Nubian queens." TK stuck his head out the window blowing kisses at all of the women that drove by. "I love you baby do your thing beautiful!" Bay pulled on the back of his shirt.

"TK get your ass back in this car." Bay laughed at how crazy TK was behaving.

"Slow down...slow down I'm about to go for mine pull up on that hoe right there." TK pointed at a woman who had a super duper stupidly put together booty that was fatter that any ass that either of them had seen in the life.

"Damn." Bay mumbled to himself while slowing down preparing to pull over so TK could talk to the woman.

"What's good ma what a nigga got to do to get some conversation?" TK sounded corny shooting his shot. The woman switched her ass a little harder TK looked at Bay with a cheesy grin on his face tapping on his arm. "She going...she going." He focused up then leaned half way out of the window and prepared to get his talk on. The lady turned around and had a mustache and a whole beard stumble. "Pull off...pull off its nigga bitch pull off Bay damn!" TK got back inside of the car at the same moment Bay increased speed. "You saw that shit?"

"Yeah I saw you on your openminded shit." Bay laughed while turning the music up louder.

"Fuck you." TK mumbled feeling embarrassed that he was lusting over a transsexual man. He shook his head Miami had some tricky shit going on he was going to stick to the bitches who he knew like Jazmine. If he met any new women while in Miami he was doing a spot check grabbing crotches on the spot. He looked over at Bay who was still laughing at him and developed a minor attitude.

## Chapter 18

"The men have arrived." Jazmine sounded thirsty and thottish she was ready to party and have a good time. Semeya was going crazy stressing over nothing. She was worried that Bay wasn't coming because only one of the tickets that she purchased were used. Semeya's eyes widened in surprise which she quickly reconciled she didn't want Jazmine to know much she was into Bay. It was too late Jazmine had peeped her happiness and excitement. Jazmine played it off like she wasn't aware of the way her cousin was feeling.

"It's open!" Jazmine yelled once she heard the guys knocking on the door.

"Girl I missed you so much." TK walked inside of the mansion and shut the door behind him. "Oh my fucking shit." TK frowned looking inside of the mansion. "What the fuck." He was taken aback he had never seen luxury in person. "People really live like this?"

"Where is Bay?" Jazmine asked before Semeya got a chance to.

"I'm sorry." TK looked at Semeya with sad puppy dog eyes and then over to Jazmine. "He said wasn't coming he had to take care of something."

"Whatever." Semeya turned around quickly to walk away or everyone would have seen her eyes tear up she was so mad at Bay. How could he be so insensitive and inconsiderate? Why did he lie to her if he didn't want to come to Miami and chill with her he could have just said that he didn't have to lie in bed making plans with her for them to spend time together with each other? Why did he lie was pussy that important to him that he would act like he was interested in her as a person if he only wanted to fuck he should have kept it real and said that. Semeya was in her feelings and when she hurried off to be by herself TK and Jazmine both identified with how much she cared about Bay and on such short notice.

"TK fuck you." Jazmine slapped him on the arm pissed off that her cousin was semi heartbroken over Bay 's dog ass.

"What the fuck I aint do shit." TK put his hands up to block any more attempts to attack him if she decided to beat on him. "What did I do?"

"You know that's fucked up what Bay did to her." Jazmine pointed in his face mushing the palm of her hand against the front of his face before walking away from him. "Fuck you don't talk to me."

"Bay is a grown man what I got to do with Bay ? He can make up his own mind up that's a grown man that don't got nothing to do with me." TK walked after Jazmine pulling at her arm trying to get her attention. He was so caught up in the argument that he was having with Jazmine that he forgot that Bay was actually standing outside waiting to be let in the house so he could surprise Semeya. Bay didn't tell TK about his plan until they got outside of the house.

"Get out of my face TK...get out of my face." Jazmine pulled her arm away from her. TK picked his phone up and read the text. "You texting bitches in my face...you know what nigga do you and I'm going to do me. You might want to find a hotel room I'm fucking somebody tonight...one of these Miami niggas is getting this New York work." Jazmine was talking reckless and disrespectfully to TK and that infuriated him.

"I knew you was nasty bitch can't take your dog ass nowhere you see niggas get dick happy. It's cool you nasty bitch I'm gon' get me some Miami bitches then some big booty Miami bitches yeah I need that. Regular job working bitches not pill selling drug dealing bitches. Real fat booty job working bitch is on the way."

"Only bitch stupid to put up with your broke ass is me and I'm tired so tonight you're on your own roam around and find you some big booty Miami bitches that like broke ass New York niggas." Jazmine tried to walk pass TK and he grabbed her by her hair.

"Jazmine I will kill you in this fucking house." TK let her hair go and caught her hand that came flying at his face Jazmine was trying to dig her nails in his face. They were about to start fighting until Bay knocked at the door. Jazmine and TK locked eyes before going to answer the door.

"You was just going to leave me outside TK?" Bay stepped inside of the house with his arms in the air. "Where is Semeya?" Bay looked around for her.

"She upstairs." Jazmine smiled realizing what Bay was up to. Bay walked away and softly walked up the stairs looking for Semeya. "I like Bay he's alright with me." Jazmine tried to take TK by the hand.

"Naw bitch we aint cool keep that same energy Miami niggas...Miami niggas somebody getting this pussy tonight." TK's jaws puffed out like a little kid he was mad as hell with Jazmine's ratchet ass saying all of that fucked up shit to him. "Who does that, who talks to their man...friend like that?"

"TK you know how I get I be saying crazy stuff, but aint nobody getting none of this good pussy except you." Jazmine walked up on him leaning her body against his then placed the palm of her hand against his chest.

"Naw...nope I aint fucking with you." TK tried to look away moving his head away from her face while she tried to plant kisses over his face he resisted her long as he could before giving and returning her kisses.

Semeya was upstairs dialing Bay 's number she frowned listening to his phone ring once he answered it. "So you didn't get on the plane?"

"No I didn't." He didn't say anything else he carefully eased along the hallway looking into each room looking for her.

"Is there a particular reason why?" Semeya wanted to be mad at him, but hearing his voice changed her entire disposition she went from being mad to wanting to be in his presence.

"I told you I got bitches and not to get in your feelings when you see me running around smashing bitches left and right." Bay stuck his tongue out he knew that he was being petty by using this time and space to tell her what she had said to him.

"Wow you did all of this to prove to me that you can sleep with bitches ok I'm hanging up now." Semeya was on the verge of hanging up.

"Why would you do that?" Bay smiled Semeya's voice was becoming clearer which meant that he was getting closer to wherever she was.

"Why are you whispering?" Semeya wasn't mad she just wasn't feeling the way the situation was playing out with Bay.

"I don't disrespect my girl." Bay had found her he stood right outside of the bedroom where Semeya was. He looked at her while biting on his bottom lip.

"Wow you got a girl now?" Semeya didn't know what else to say to him after hearing him admit that he had a significant other she hung up the phone feeling sad. She had gone through all sorts of trouble to make things perfect for Bay so he and she could spend some time together.

"Just like that...you aint even gon' put up a fight for a nigga?" Bay stepped inside of the room making his presence known. Semeya turned around and put her hands over her face to hide her happiness as she blushed.

"Nope...no...no." She put her hands up to block his sight into her face she didn't want him to see her gushing Semeya turned around and tried to flee inside of the bathroom long enough to get herself together. Bay grabbed her and pulled her into him. "No...nope let me go."

"It's cool to like me I'm a lovable dude." Bay kissed on her ear and then hugged her tight as he could. "You know I wouldn't miss an opportunity to be with my baby."

"I'm your baby now?" Semeya rolled her eyes while smiling ear to ear.

"Always and forever you make a mother fucker want to sing." Bay copied Martin Lawrence's character Bilal in the movie house party.

"Shut up." Semeya screeched as Bay tossed her on the bed.

"I say all the right words to get inside of your panties." Bay said playfully while pulling her pants down her legs so he could climb on top of her.

"I don't have on any panties." Semeya lay flat on her back in the bed with both of her hands over her face hiding her feelings.

"Good." Bay opened her legs and put his mouth on top of her opening.

## Chapter 19

Bay lay in bed thinking about Semeya and how much he was digging her. Semeya entered into his life and captured his heart and held it for ransom. She had no intention to give it back he wasn't sure if he wanted it back. Bay shook his head he was falling fast and was helpless to himself regain control of his emotions. He was too far gone and he knew better than to get wrapped up too soon because love didn't love anyone that was one of the lies that he told himself as a defense mechanism. His last relationship ended horribly leaving him with a severely broken heart and a bitter taste in his mouth as far as love was concerned. He was emotionally guarded with a huge stonewall securely installed around his heart. Semeya was slowly deconstructing his fortress piece by piece. He didn't want her to have so much control over him. It upset him whenever he saw her and his face lit up with undeniable happiness. Bay looked over to his side where Semeya rested with her eyes closed. He stood up and walked over to the window looking out into the night peering at the beach. Before long he was dressed and easing out of the mansion and onto the beach where he intended to sit, watching waves, and figuring out what's going on inside of his head. It didn't take long for Bay to find a spot to plopped down at. He pulled his knees up to his chest and put his chin down on his knees.

Thinking over his life and all of his toxic relationships that had a negative impact on him and his life. Loving the wrong women had him falsely assuming every woman was argumentative, disloyal, manipulative, and money hungry. Bay hadn't had any meaningful relationships in his life since breaking up with Kristi. He opened himself up allowing his vulnerability to shine through like a fool. Kristi was an Instagram hoe who slept with anybody who had a couple of dollars to give to her by the time that Bay found out it was too late he was heavily invested in her and in love with her. He didn't want to revisit the type of pain that Kristi brought into his life. Past hurt and incident from years ago had Bay contemplating hopping on a plane and flying home while Semeya slept othe than that he was a goner trapped by her and imprisoned by the feeling that she was awakening in him.

"Are you going to make this a habit, running out on me when I'm not looking?" Semeya squatted down behind Bay then she scooted right up on him until her breast were pressed against back. She hugged him from behind and squeezed him lovingly. Bay lowered his head in defeat there was no way in hell he would be able to walk away from Semeya.

"Running isn't in my protocol." Bay stuck his foot further into his mouth he wanted to smack the palm of his hand against his forehead why was he speaking to her like there was a real possibility of them being together? She belonged to Jahlil.

"I can't tell." Semeya referenced an incident while they were having sex when Bay was overjoyed with pleasure and had to roll away from Semeya to escape her clutches.

"I needed some fresh air and time to think about." Bay couldn't find the right words to express what he was going through so he went quiet.

"Time to think about what?" Semeya wondered if he was as confused as she was? She swayed side to side softly before nudging him on his side. "You not going to talk to me?"

"If I told you that I'm falling in love with you and I can't get enough of you. What if I said I yearn for you to touch me, what would you say?" Bay shut his eyes in disbelief he couldn't believe that he was being so open with Semeya.

"I would say I'm just as confused." Semeya didn't know how to correctly answer Bay's question because she wasn't thinking straight either. Jahlil was her man and she wasn't thinking about him or how complicated things would be when he returned. She wasn't worried about him popping up and catching her with Bay she didn't plan and think ahead she would cross that bridge when the time came.

"This is some scary shit." Bay felt tears watering up inside of his eye ducts. He had been carrying around so much hurt and pain, disappointment, frustration, and resentment inside of his heart that he wasn't living a full life he was squandering his life away peddling petty drugs and shooting men of a lesser statue then him. He had no other choices the ghetto was what it was and he was a product of environment survival was an everyday job that he couldn't afford to take a day off from. Being around Semeya was opening him up so wide that he had no other option other than releasing his embarrassment of past failed relationships. He had to if he needed the room for all of the emotions that Semeya were filling him with.

"What's scary?"

"Loving women." Bay wasn't aware that his response frightened Semeya.

"Do you love men?" She doubled checked questioning his sexuality in a polite manner with a single sentence.

"No...hell naw what I'm saying is I've been through a lot with women and I'm not willing to go through anymore of it. I can't take that shit I don't know how I was able to survive the shit that I survived this far. Then you and Jahlil are in love where does that leave me? You probably don't even think of me like that you probably just need a boy toy a fuck machine or something like that." Bay wasn't sure what was happening in his life he didn't recognize the man who he was becoming, love had taken over his interior forever changing him.

"I won't hurt you I'll treat you how I want to be treated, but that goes both ways if at any time you try to play me the deal is off and it's everybody for themselves. I'll protect me and you protect you" Semeya kissed on Bay's neck.

"Sounds like a good deal." Bay smiled unsure why he was believing Semeya it wasn't like she was incapable of lying. She could easily be selling him a dose of hahahaha you stupid mother fucker. "It's just one more thing. What in the hell makes you think that I trust you?"

"You don't got a choice I hold all the keys."

"Who told you that?" Bay's eyes stretched upward in surprise as Semeya palmed his balls through his shorts. "Oh." Bay's reaction made Semeya laugh. "You just might be right."

# Chapter 20

Jazmine switched sexily up to the house authoritatively moving at a nice speed she carried her shoes in her hands. Anyone watching her would assume that she was tipsy and coming home after a night of getting her swerve her on. To those who knew her It wasn't hard to tell that she and TK had been involved in some sort of scuffle. Jazmine was furious and on the verge of exploding.

"I wonder what happened?" Semeya and sat on the beach looking back at Jazmine.

"I don't know we should find out TK's ass might be in jail." Bay didn't want to move he wanted to stay wrapped up in the warmth of Semeya's loving embrace. He had to check on his cousin.

"Why do you think he might be in jail?" Semeya stood up and dusted the sand off of her butt and Bay did the same thing.

"I know my cousin and TK being some stupid ass shit." Bay was sad to inform her on how badly TK acted.

"Yeah we should see." Semeya and Bay walked over to where Jazmine was. "Jazmine!" Semeya called out to her. Hearing Semeya's voice Jazmine turned in the direction where her voice came from. She sighed frustratedly soon as she saw Semeya and Bay. "What happened?" Semeya asked walking up on Jazmine.

"Girl." Jazmine couldn't speak she didn't have the right words to convey her feelings confusion entered into her eyes, then sadness, then anger Jazmine steadied her nerves for a second then she put her hands on her hip before putting the palm of her hand upright while holding her lips inside of her mouth. She looked away from Semeya. "I am so embarrassed, my mother fucking head hurts, I done been slammed, I done got punched, my phone is gone, and girl." Jazmine inhaled deeply.

"TK did all of that?" Semeya knew that Jazmine and TK fought regularly she just never known for him to go hard like that.

"He had it done to us.":

"See what I'm saying...see what I'm saying she always want to tell my part." TK walked up to the house shirtless patting his hand against his bare chest. "She don't never want to tell her part it's always TK's fault its never nothing that she did. Its always TK...Tk....TK....TK that's all the fuck I hear is TK...TK...Tk."

"That's your name stupid!" Jazmine frowned and yelled at TK.

"I'm stupid now...I'm stupid because you want to be fucking with niggas?" TK Frowned quickly transitioning into anger filled emotions.

"I told you the nigga stopped me and said hey you have a nice look I'm shooting a movie you should come by and audition for a role."

"The nigga told you right there in your face that he wants to fuck and you was going for it sitting up there giggling with another nigga in my face."

"When did I say that he said star in a porn movie?" Jazmine put her hand out waiting for him to answer her.

"Jazmine you're not even fine like that...you're fine, but fine...fine...fine movie star fine stop playing with me Jazmine you was trying to fuck that nigga." TK was convinced that he was right in his logic and there wasn't any other alternative except for the one he concluded.

"TK shut up."

"What happened?" Semeya intervened trying to get the two of them to stop arguing long enough to finish telling what happened.

"Stupid ass TK ran across the club and dove over the table like he was a wrestler and landed on four people. They all fell to the floor he got up trying to fight the guy who said he was a movie producer and the rest of them niggas beat his ass up in there."

"They jumped me." TK defended his honor he was a punk and he didn't just get his ass beat easily as Jazmine was making it seem.

"I said they jumped you."

"Soon as I got up I went for mine got them niggas back shiiiidd I aint going." TK was proud of himself.

"No you didn't you start fighting with the wrong people." Jazmine rolled her eyes she had been drinking she wasn't as drunk as TK was she know what she saw and she saw TK get up chase after somebody who happened to be bouncer doing his job he was escorting one of the people who jumped TK out of the club when TK rushed him. "TK punched the bouncer in the face a man who is three times his size. He picked TK up and then slammed him before punching him in the face. His bouncer friends jumped in and they were punching and kicking TK. I ran over there like no that's my brother."

"She wasn't trying to fuck nobody, but I'm her brother I don't even look like you." TK shook his head thinking that Jazmine was trying to play him by being slick. He was convinced that she was trying to fuck one of those Miami niggas.

"I'm trying to help him and somebody gets to wailing upside my head I turn around and it's a whole nigga fighting me like nigga what?" Jazmine looked at Semeya in disbelief niggas had gone too far since when did niggas fight on bitches all hard like that? They tossed us out of the club then the same nigga who was fighting me comes out and slams my clutch on the ground and throws my phone so hard and far away like he never wants to see it again meanwhile TK is getting beat up by two bouncers then we came here."

" We didn't come here you left me I had to get an uber."

"You needed to be left." Jazmine walked off and into the house.

"She just mad because she was trying to fuck somebody and I fucked it up I don't care I like fucking your shit up."

"How you know she was trying to fuck TK?" Semeya enjoyed watching the craziness of Jazmine's and TK's unofficial relationship play out.

"That's what she was saying earlier in the house oh I'm fucking somebody tonight one of these Miami niggas about to get it." TK sounded ratchet and hood rattish. Semeya laughed at his silliness.

"TK is you out here talking about me?" Jazmine appeared in the doorway of the house.

"Whatever I'm saying is coming out of TK's mouth meaning I can say what the fuck I feel like saying."

"TK I will bust your head open with this bottle keep playing with me." Jazmine came charging out of the house and TK took off running with Jazmine running after him. "Keep playing with me TK!"

"Keep playing with me TK." He mocked her while running away from her.

"We better not ever get like that I will leave your crazy ass the fuck alone." Bay looked at Semeya and then down the beach where Jazmine chased TK.

"They are in love I'll take some of that everyday in America." Semeya laughed taking Bay by the hand and looking sheepishly into his eyes. "We might as well after all we're in Miami."

"We can't get upstairs fast enough." Bay and Semeya walked into the house hand in hand on their way upstairs into the bedroom where they were about to engage in the most x rated uncensored hot and steamy dick terrorizing coochie sex imaginable.

# Chapter 21

Jahlil was in Miami on business he came through to pick up an Instagram modeling chick who he had been messaging for a few months. The opportunity had arrived where he had time to entertain her. He was on his way to the airport where a private flight awaited him. He had Cynthia aka Cyn the body on Instagram riding shotgun with him when he realized that he hadn't spoken to Semeya in a few days he pulled over at a gas station and called her during the process of paying for and then pumping gas.

"What are you doing Lil Baby?" Jahlil stood arrogantly at the counter looking at the cashiers or whatever positions they held in their lowly professions with disdain and contempt in his eyes. He didn't want to do any unnecessary talking to the humble servants he only wanted them to serve him so that he could be gone about his business.

"Sir you can't use your phone at the counter." The short thick neck semi ugly dark skin girl with a fucked up hairdo said looking at him impatiently. She looked like she rolled out of bed didn't bother brushing her teeth or getting herself together and just brought her funky pussy ass self to work without any care for anyone in her work atmosphere especially the paying customers.

"What's your name?" Jahlil looked at the girl with disrespectful eyes.

"Kayla." She blinked at him unflinchingly.

"I know you may hear this a lot you ugly as fuck so stop flirting with me and do your job." Jahlil went back to talking to Semeya like he hadn't just emotionally wounded another human being.

"I'm going to have to ask you to leave sir."

"Bitch I aint going nowhere without my gas. I don't think you know who I am. I'm a rich ass out of your league ass nigga. I'm a better nigga than your daddy ass nigga. I got so much mother fucking money white people respect it. I got enough power and influence to have a man sitting out there all day until you get out of work and then do something to you if I wanted to. I'm not going to do that because you ugly you bad built you possibly stank so I forgive you...you're probably feeling sorry for yourself. Now take this money, press that button, and give me my mother fucking gas or you can go get that buck tooth goofy ass looking white boy to do it for you."

"First off all mother fucker." Kayla looked up and saw the three men who were with Jahlil all pulling guns out and aiming them at her. Jahlil stood there arrogantly.

"Now I need your store cameras and for that white boy to pump my gas. Hurry up little ugly." Jahlil pointed at the white boy who was behind the counter with the girl and his goons raced behind the counter and snatched him up by force before taking him out to the cars where he filled every single tank up on every car that rode with Jahlil. "Yeah baby had to check some ugly ass dark skin thirsty looking ass bitch who looks like she needs to do favors for niggas to get some dick. Fuck me and I'll give you some free gas ass bitch." Jahlil said everything that he had to say in front of Kayla he wanted to hurt her feelings and teach her dog face ass some manners about getting out of line with real rich niggas.

"I know how you go my baby always flexing his nuts." Semeya shook her head while making the bed up preparing to mess it up with Bay in a few minutes. "Where you at?"

"On my way to LA where you at?" '

"In Miami with Jazmine and TK they been fighting and acting crazy the whole time."

"Where at in Miami Lil Baby?" Semeya told him where she was thinking it wouldn't matter one way or the other because he was on his way to LA and she had nothing to worry about.

"Why you're about to pull up on me?" Semeya asked playfully.

"Never know you never could tell what I'm gon' do. I'm about to get up out of here but keep it light Lil Baby." Jahlil hung up the phone he rarely ever told Semeya that he loved her or called her by her name. He called her Lil Baby and said keep it light instead of I love you. "Yo ya'll come we got to make another stop.

I'm going to pop in on Lil Baby and surprise her I know she can't wait to see me." Jahlil smiled arrogantly before getting into his car and pulling off.

## Chapter 22

"I'm gon' kill you Jazmine I swear you gon make me kill you." TK and Jazmine were butt ass naked outside in the backyard by the pool in a chair having sex. Jazmine was turned around in a doggystyle position and TK was standing behind her pulling on her long braids. "Bitch you gon' make me kill somebody." TK groaned out while stroking his hips around digging Jazmine's back out. Jazmine's back was arched so that she her ass was fully accessible to him. TK held onto her hips winding away. "Jazmine on my momma I'm gon' kill you bitch you better not never give this pussy to nobody but me bitch."

"TK shut up." Jazmine moaned out.

"You think I'm playing with you bitch I will kill you." He pulled her braids tighter and stroked harder digging deeper and Jazmine loved it.

"I don't believe you." She antagonized him making him stroke faster and harder until they were galloping and fucking at the same time. Jazmine loved Tk's stupid ass and he loved her they weren't toxic to each other for the simple fact that they both were hoes and did whatever they wanted to do whenever they wanted to do it. They had great sex together neither one of them wanted to be honest about how they felt toward the other. They were in love and couldn't deny it but couldn't accept it either.

"I'm gon' whoop that ass Jazmine I'm not fucking around don't play bitch." TK held onto Jazmine and kept stroking. "Jazz come ride this dick." TK was getting tired and needed her to take over while he caught his breath.

"Shut your ass up don't tell me what to do." Jazmine snatched her arm away from TK while getting up then waiting for him to sit down so she could climb up on top of him.

"There it go sit on down get comfortable." The look in TK's eyes made Jazmine laugh.

"You aint got to look like that." Jazmine eased down on top of his erection before licking her tongue across his lips and then slipped her tongue deep into his mouth.

***

Tk and Jazmine were exhausted and lying beside each other on the side of the pool their love making had gotten so freaky and out of hand they ended up in the grass rolling around.

"I think my side hurt." TK put his hand on his side he was starting to sober up.

"You got a cramp want me to rub it for you?" Jazmine reached for his side.

"I think one of those niggas cracked one of my ribs when they was kicking me." All of the drugs that TK had consumed were wearing off and he was returning back to normal. Everything he wasn't able to feel while under the influence of alcohol and drugs were coming to the forefront of his brain as certain parts of his body started throbbing. "My eye is starting to hurt and shit." TK sat up in pain he picked up his clothes and put them on before walking into the mansion.

"TK are you alright?" Jazmine walked behind him following him into the house. She wanted to laugh first she had to make sure that he wasn't seriously injured before laughing.

"Hell naw I need to go to sleep." TK limped over to the couch and laid down. He pulled out a few pills and popped them he wanted to be high and unable to feel anything.

"Need me to take care of you?" Jazmine sat down next to TK. He got up baby I need to lay on the floor this couch is too soft and it's hurting my body. TK got up and laid down on the floor. Jazmine lay beside him flat out right there on the floor she popped a few more pills.

\*\*\*

Upstairs Semeya was on top of Bay giving him the business his toes crunched up and twitched around as he bit down on his lip and tried to hold on long as he could. Semeya leaned over and kissed him before running her tongue against his cheek and then along his neck. Bay lay underneath Semeya completely under her spell her body was giving his so much pleasure that he had to grit his teeth trying to stall his seed from spilling prematurely. Bay wasn't willing to let Semeya off the hook so easily he needed her body it felt good to him swimming around inside of her moisture, but he had to get from underneath her or else it was wrap. Bay rolled over on top of her and pressed his fist into the mattress on each side of her head and pumped hard and forceful strokes that entered inside of her body at an even and controlled pace. Bay had his lip tucked inside of his mouth grinding his teeth against his bottom lip while focusing on making Semeya cum. He worked her body so good that Semeya looked at him with confusion in her eyes like she didn't know who he was or what he was trying to do to her body. She had made love to Bay a few times but the man on top of her tonight was fresh on the scene he was taking her body through unfamiliar changes and deliberately socking it to her unconcerned with the consequences of loving someone down so effectively. Bay was on some shit and using his entire body to fuck the happiness out of Semeya his strokes came from his neck, his shoulders, back, pelvis, and thigh muscles he put everything he had into each stroke using the force from his legs that came from grinding his toes into the floor he wanted to wax Semeya's ass and give her everything that she gave him which was feelings of completion, unlimited happiness, he wanted to make her question everything that she knew about life and love the same way she was doing to him just by being present in his life.

"Let it go baby bust it...bust it...bust that nut baby bust that nut." Bay held the top of Semeya's shoulders inside the palm of his hands. He wiggled his waist around moving his dick around just enough to be felt. Semeya was coming her legs reacted differently like they belonged to two different people. Her right leg shook and jerked and her left leg kicked out straight and remained in the air while her toes quivered. Bay felt good inside of her he made her body cream he pushed her beyond the limit of her comfortability. Semeay was in her feelings at home in her relationship with Jahlil she was pampered and well taken care of. Jahlil was a great provider and supporter. In the sexual department she hadn't bust a nut as a result from feeling a warm dick attached to a flesh and blood person fucking with Jahlil. Since she met Bay he was consistently making her cum in her panties, down the fullness of his shaft, and on the interior of his tongue. Bay treated her body like he was safeguarded with administering pleasure to it "Let me get mine baby...there it go...there it go." Bay released everything that he had pent up inside of him right into her body and nether one of them seem to care that they weren't using a condom.

## Chapter 22

"It should be somewhere around here I haven't been here before the GPS says we are right here. It should be somewhere around here." Jahlil sucked his teeth he pulled up in front of the mansion where Semeya was staying. "It's right here." Jahlil got out of his car and called Semeya's phone the phone rang until it went to voice mail that was odd and unlike Semeya no matter what she was doing she made it her business to answer the phone whenever Jahlil called her. He hung up the phone and called her right back giving her time to redeem herself maybe she was in the tub or doing something else that was distracting her that was understandable he called back giving her a chance to answer the phone before he got mad and developed an attitude. He didn't mind getting on shit if he felt like someone was playing him for a fool. The phone went to voicemail again after ringing several times. Jahlil walked up to the door and turned the knob to his surprise it was unlocked. He walked into the front door.

He looked around the first thing he smelt was alcohol. Jahlil shook his head automatically assuming that Jazmine was entirely the blame for the place reeking of alcohol. Semeya partied not like Jazmine did and if Semeya did anything fucked up in life Jazmine had a lot to do with it. Jahlil walked pass the living briefly looking into it if he would have stepped inside just a little further he would have seen Jazmine and TK sprawled out on the floor. He walked until he reached the kitchen then he frowned wondering where the hell could Semeya be. "Lil Baby!" Jahlil called out for her as he ascended the stairs. "Lil Baby."

***

"Holy shit." Semeya hopped up out of bed quickly putting her clothes on she recognized that voice anywhere she heard it.

"What's up?" Bay sat up semi dazed and partially asleep. He looked at her.

"Jahlil is here." She whispered.

"What?" He wasn't sure that he heard her correctly.

"Jahlil is here." She ran around the room uncertain what to do until finally she ran into the bathroom and ran some bathwater. Bay got dressed and cut the light out. He looked around the room for a weapon in case things got out of hand. How could he explain being in darkened bedroom with this man's woman at such a late hour? What could he say and what would be believable not a damn thing and that was exactly why Bay was searching around the room for something to bust this nigga's ass. He knew he should have driven to Miami that way he could have had his gun on him instead of his ass in one hand and his dick in the other.

"Lil Baby." Jahlil's voice was coming closer and closer and Bay was running out of options quick fast and in a hurry. Jahlil kept a gun on him and he had several people with him who kept guns on them so not only was Bay outnumbered he was also outgunned. He felt the walls closing in on him as paranoia set in. This nigga was going to kill him Semeya was too fine to let go that pussy was too juicy to let another nigga have her without a fight and she was just an overall dope individual Semeya was that bitch. Loyal down to earth smart educated patient loving considerate and everything a woman would want her son get from a wife. Bay recognized that and respected her and all of her splendor, but he still didn't feel like dying about a bitch no matter how exclusively fantastic she was he still valued his life. He had to do something and fast, but what he ran out of options the bedroom door opened and Jahlil walked in.

"Lil Baby you in here!" He called out again. Lil Baby." Jahlil walked toward the bathroom calling out for Semeya then he stopped and inhaled deeply as he could. He was the smartest person in the world but according to his sense of smell somebody had just finished fucking up storm in this bedroom. He paused for a second then turned to face the bed to his surprise it was made up perfectly that was the second Semeya did after putting her clothes back on. "This might be a trick let me double check so I can know that way I won't be tripping over some ole bullshit." Jahlil walked over to the bed and reached his hands out prepared to feel the sheets and blanket to see if they were damp from intense love making before he could he heard a noise something fell and he looked up in time to see a shadowy figure charging at him with something in his hands. Jahlil tried to reach for his gun, but Bay struck first. A loud thud sounding noise stun Jahlil causing him to fall over on the bed he stood up and stumbled backward. He shook his head clearing his vision and reached for his gun a second time and this time Jahlil fell down to his knees and keeled over onto the floor. Bay stood over him holding onto a metal object.

"Oh shit Bay what have you done, did you kill him?" Semeya's eyes bulged out in a frantic. Fear gripped her heart and made it impossible for her to move.

"He's not dead he's unconscious I knocked him out. We can't worry about that we have to act fast."

"Act fast and do what?" Semeya looked up at Bay wondering what kind of thoughts were racing around his mind?

"I'm sorry baby." Bay lowered his eyes and shook his head.

"Sorry for what, what is you talking about?"

"Forgive me." Bay backhanded Semeya so hard that she collapsed to the floor. Bay moved quickly searching the room until he found a sharp pair of scissors then he yanked the sheets off of the bed and cut them up into long strips that could be used to bind people's hands and feet together. Bay tied Jahlil up first, ran his pockets, relieved him of his money, then he did the same thing to Semeya. Bay looked down at Semeya for a few more seconds before leaning down kissing her softly on the lips then he hurried down the stairs where he walked over to Jazmine and TK sleeping on the floor and tied the two of them up together then he robbed them. Bay walked smoothly out of the backdoor and continued down the trail until he reached the rental car that he and TK rode in. Bay started the car up and drove smoothly away without any further incidents.

## Chapter 23

Jahlil blinked then opened his eyes his vision was slightly blurred he shook his head around to loosen the dizziness that encircled his head. A tingling sensation throbbed onside of Jahlil's head . He looked around realizing that he was lying on the floor with his hands and feet tied behind his back. He struggled to free himself he grunted while  trying to yank his arms free. "What the fuck is this is shit?"

"Jahlil." Semya called out his name weakly her face and head was sore from being slapped unconscious.

She couldn't wait to get home she was gon' cuss Bay's ignorant ass out. Where did he get off doing some shit like that? She wasn't the one she didn't allow men to put their hands on her and get away with it. Oh hell naw that nigga had gone too far.

"Little Baby you good?" Jahlil wasn't afraid he was used to the drama and violence associated with the streets  robbery was a part of his lifestyle. He had been on both sides of the gun, when things were fucked up for him and he was down bad and out on his ass and was thirsty for a come up he  pulled his gun out on plenty niggas and got away with their shit. When he came into some money he pulled out his pistol and made niggas understand that he wanted his money in a worse way in fact way worse then they wanted it. Jahlil was ready to die over his money, family, respect, and would willingly kill to protect all three.

"I'm alright." Semeya lied denying her pain physically she suffered minor injuries ranging from a tiny knot onside of her head from where Bay's hand connected. The bulk of her hurt was emotional.  She felt that Bay was a common street punk scheming on a come up and scammed her. Jahlil warned her about niggas pretending to want her , but really were interested in kidnapping her and then holding her for ransom. She never thought Bay was one of those type of people. He touched her body so deliberately and delicate. When they were around each other the signs of new love was obvious. More importantly she felt it in her gut. A woman's intuition was a built in compass that helped her navigate through the wilderness of life. Semyea felt it in her heart that Bay loved her if that was the case then why would he hit her in the first place?

"Little baby roll over here to me and put your back against mine so we can untie each other." Jahlil continued to talk and coach Semeya how to roll over to him. "That's it Little baby try to sit up." Jahlil watched Semeya rolling over to him. Once she leaned up against him he moved his fingers around feeling to see what type of knot the robber used to bind them. Jahlil worked on untying the shredded sheets from Semeya's wrists. He was semi impressed with the knots whoever tied them was a dope boy who pulled a couple of home invasions in the process of getting back on his feet. He could tell because the knot was tied too tight it was tight enough to hold them long enough for him to escape. After he got away he wanted them to be able to untie themselves so if no one came by the house and found them they wouldn't starve to death while waiting for somebody to find them they would be able to untie themselves. "Sit still Little baby I almost got this knot untied."

"Ok." Semeya answered him, but her mind was occupied with unanswered questions, different scenarios and ways that Bay could have handled the situation. Semeya's eyes brightened when she felt that her hand were able to move.

"Go get a knife and cut me loose Little baby." Jahlil called out and Semeya removed the makeshift rope from her feet then she hurried downstairs and came back within a short time and cut Jahlil free. "Is there anybody else in the house?"

"Jazmine and TK, but they should be in their room down the hall."

"Aint nobody in that room that I checked all of those rooms before I got to this one." Jahlil got up from the floor. "Is there anybody else in here?"

"No." Semeya shook her head.

"You got your dildo with you?" Jahlil wanted to address the fact that he smelled sex when he walked inside of the room. He didn't want to come right out and say bitch you was up in here fucking somebody so he used a smoother approach and method to ask the same question without making it sound like what it was.

"It's in the bathroom." Semeya got up and walked into the bathroom and returned with her dildo in hand the one that she stuck against the wall and fucked doggy style.

"Damn freak." Jahlil smiled then turned away his happiness came from being tricked he felt a huge wave of relief wash over him when he saw Semya holding her dildo in hand. "Come on Little baby I'm not leaving you in Miami by yourself."

"I don't feel safe here anymore anyway." Semeya lied she wondered where Bay had run off too?

***

"TK how is we tied up?" Jazmine moved around trying to untie TK so he could untie her.

"Jazmine I guess this is my fault too. This aint got nothing to do with these Miami niggas that you was fucking with." TK sucked his teeth. "Bitch done got us robbed." TK sighed deeply automatically thinking that Jazmine had gotten them into some bullshit trying to be cute fucking around with some cutthroat ass niggas.

"TK how is this my fault?"

"Whatever man." TK rolled his eyes. "Always doing some shit man."

"If you wouldn't have punched him in the face we wouldn't be here and we don't even know if those are the same people who robbed us. It could have been the uber driver I told him that we were here on vacation."

"Why would you do that, why would you tell these dirty south mother fuckers that we was tourists you got us robbed Jazmine."

"Calm down because you don't got no money to get robbed for." Jazmine was growing tired of TK talking shit to her he needed to be focusing on how they were going to get out of the ropes that had them tied together.

"I got my life Jazmine bitch my life is more than money. My life is precious my life is priceless Jazmine."

"To who TK?"

"To me bitch." TK got offended and sucked his teeth. "Remember that...remember that." TK shook his head. He was pissed off he felt like Jazmine wasn't showing him enough affection she acted like his life didn't mean shit when it came to money.

"Jazmine...TK." Semeya called out their names in surprise and raced over to where they were tied up at. She quickly untied them.

"Semeya he done got us robbed I told you that nigga wasn't no movie producer they followed us back to the house and got our asses because of this bitch." TK. Jazmine had heard enough of TK talking shit and degrading her soon as the ropes came off Jazmine got up and punched her fists down on top of TK's head.

"I'm tired of you fucking with me TK!" Jazmine pushed him in the back and walked away from him. Jahlil stood back watching them he chuckled to himself. Jazmine and TK was a joke to him. Jazmine would forever be a freak bitch from the booed to him and TK was a sucker ass nigga for one he was booed up with Jazmine and for two he let niggas beat his ass then tied him and his woman up. Now that he was free he wasn't mad seeking revenge over even thinking about it.

"I'm riding back with Jahlil Jazmine you have to take the rental car back I'll meet ya'll at the airport."

"No she'll meet you two at home she's riding on the jet with me." Jahlil said putting to rest any misconceptions pertaining to Semeya.

"Yo you see that do you see how that nigga just told her some shit and she didn't call him bitch ass nigga or tell him shut up or get the fuck out of her face, why you can't respect me like that?" TK got in Jazmine's face.

"TK I'm not playing with you get the fuck out of my face." Jazmine bawled her fist up prepared to punch him.

"See what I'm saying fucking ignorant."

"I'll be in the car." Jahlil couldn't take anymore of Jazmine and TK. He walked away and out of the house. Jazmine looked at Semeya and shrugged her shoulders and used her eyes to ask her where is Bay? Semeya shook her head letting her know that she had the slightest idea where he was at, but the look in Semeya's face was one of pure sadness. Jazmine recognized that her cousin was hurting and it had everything to do with Bay.

## Chapter 24

Back home Bay paced his living room floor stressing hard he had called Semeya every hour since had been home and wasn't able to get in touch with her. He hoped that she was alright he had hit her pretty hard and hoped that she understood that he did what he had to do. The tension was thick and Jahlil was right there he had to bust a move on the spot. That was the best play that he could put down. Bay pulled called Jazmine and TK's phones each one of them went directly to voice mail. Bay tried to hit Semeya up on Facebook and frowned in disbelief when he found out that she had blocked him. He went to her instagram and learned that he had been deleted there as well. He went to snapchat and got the same result. This nigga Jahlil must have found out about them and if that was the case what was Jahlil gearing up to do to him? Bay grabbed his strap and put hit on his waist before walkling out of his front door. He hopped in his car to spin a few corners while sorting things out in his mind then he was going to Jazmine's house and get some answers.

Bay pulled up at Jazmine's house and got out of his car. He opened his trunk and pulled out a black plastic bag. He walked into Jazmine's house.

"What up Jazmine?" He reached into the bag searching around until he pulled out a brown paper bag with her name written across it. He handed it to her. Jazmine's face lit up in the cheesiest smile. She wasn't smiling for her little bit of money back she was happy that Semeya was totally wrong about Bay. He wasn't robbing them for his personal benefit he took the money as a decoy while he got away and he didn't want to blow up Semeya and have her going through it with Jahlil. Semeya was under the impression that Bay had robbed them for the money because Jahlil had fifty thousand dollars in his pocket that night. "Where TK at?"

"TK!" Jazmine yelled out and TK came out of the kitchen with a frown on his face. He had on a white t shirt that had seen better days with a big wet stain on the front of it. "You know I'm trying to wash these fucking dishes what you want? Aye nigga." He smiled once he saw Bay. "I told Jazmine you got paper and you wasn't trying to rob Jahlil that's what Semeya thinks you was fucking with her just to get next to Jahlil."

"Damn TK I thought it was nigga up in my kitchen." Jazmine didn't want TK to spill the tea she wanted Bay to at least think about what he did to make Semeya so mad at him.

"Why would she think I would use her to rob Jahlil?" The look in Bay's face was all the evidence that Jazmine needed to see. Looking at Bay she saw a man who was in love and would do anything for the woman he loved. "We was in the moment...the nigga was right there she was in the bathroom naked and he was sniffing in the air he knew what was up I had to put a different thought in his head. Shit just happened so fast before I knew it I was tying niggas up and fleeing the scene. I still got everybody's shit right here." He reached in his pocket and pulled out three hundred dollars. "This is yours."

"I thought you said you had twenty eight dollars TK?" Jazmine counted the money with Bay as he peeled it off of his bankroll.

"Naw he really had twenty five dollars I just feel like a grown man should have more money than that in his pocket." Bay laughed at her then held his hand out waiting for TK to take the money.

"I told you." TK wiped his hands on the side of his jeans then reached out for the money.

"Now you can pay me back for paying your phone bill." Jazmine held her hand out not expecting to be paid TK's broke ass wasn't about to part with one dollar of that money.

"Damn Jazmine I just got this money you don't want me to have shit damn why you so money hungry. Damn you sweating me for sixty dollars. I don't ask you for shit when I'm watching your kids for free, doing homework for free, washing dishes, cooking, and yardwork for free."

"You get pussy for free...you get food for free...you live her, shower, shave, shit, and watch cable t.v. for free. You talk on your phone for free." Jazmine yelled back at him.

"See there now you fronting because I live with my mother I just be over here." TK was dead ass serious in his logic he was right and Jazmine was wrong.

"Keep your money TK." Jazmine gave him a strong objective look before poking her lips out.

"What's all that you got an attitude I don't give a fuck so what get mad I'm not about to just give you my money you."

"Give me your money I'm stupid." Jazmine repeated the parts of TK's conversation that pissed her off.

"You know what take the fucking money Jazmine. I only had twenty eight dollars so now I got one hundred." He handed Jazmine two one hundred dollar bills and Jazmine took it then put it in her bra. "Jazmine you're really going to take my money?" TK looked devastated. "So money hungry." TK looked at Jazmine thinking she was going to give him his money back when she didn't he sigh before walking off. "Let me wash these dishes before I beat this bitch ass."

"Ya'll niggas is crazy." Bay laughed at Jazmine and TK then he got serious. "Yo what's up with your cousin she's bullshitting she know what's up I need her."

"Did you call her?"

"You know she blocked me on everything." Bay thought that Semeya told Jazmine what was going on between them.

"She really didn't tell me that." Jazmine had a blank look on her face she was at a loss for words she wasn't aware that Semeya was that deep in her feelings. "I'll call her for you." Jazmine dialed Semeya's number.

"What you doing?" Semeya answered the phone on the first ring.

"You must be bored you answered the phone all fast and shit?" Jazmine chuckled.

"No on my way to Sam's Club to pick up a few things." Semeya walked out of her front door and got into her car.

"You talk to Bay yet?" Jazmine shrugged her shoulders preparing herself for whatever came out of Semeya's mouth.

"Hell naw and I aint he know what he did."

"He brought everything here I don't think it was ever about the money."

"How do you know?" Semeya felt her lips ease into a small smile she wasn't ready to leave Bay alone he was her thug fantasy and the reason that she smiled so hard whenever she was home alone lying in bed reminiscing.

"He gave back fifty thousand dollars for you that says a lot. He's here now and he wants to talk to you."

"No I don't want to talk to him." Semeya called out hoping she wasn't too late which she was Jazmine had already given him the phone.

"Why not, why you don't want to talk to me?" The sound of Bay's voice sent familiar chills dancing up her spine. Semeya didn't know what to say to him her head no longer hurt she did, however still have traces of a black eye. She hung up the phone unsure why. "This bitch is crazy." Bay smiled then chuckled before handing Jazmine her phone back.

"At least you know that she'll be at Sam's Club." Jazmine shrugged her shoulders then shook her head like it's up to you now.

"What I'm supposed to run up in Sam's Club on some white people shit hold on honey let me talk to you?" The look in Bay's eyes let her know that he wasn't going to do anything like that it wasn't his style.

"That's not white people shit that's what people in love that's called letting her know that she matters and you're willing to go above and beyond for her shit."

"What is she gon' do for me?" Bay wondered out loud.

"Forgive you I don't know what else to say to you I done told you all that I could the rest is up to you."

"Sss what ya'll doing tonight?" Bay asked just to change the flow of their words.

"Shit aint doing nothing at all we have gotten accustomed to double dating so if Semeya aint with you I don't know what to say." Jazmine let him know that she wasn't doing anything with him then she pulled out her Sam's Club card and held it out for him to take.

"I see what you're doing." Bay snatched the card out of her hand then turned and walked out the house with a big smile on his face.

***

Twenty minutes later he was feeling like a sucker sitting inside of Samn's Club's parking lot. He got out of his car and walked into the store. He grabbed a shopping cart knowing damn well he didn't intend to buy shit. He walked around the store slowly feeling like a baby stalker as he searched the isles looking for Semeya. "Shit there that bitch go." Bay's eyes widened and he felt his breath get caught up in his throat making it hard for him to breathe. What the hell was going on what was happening to his body. He had to pull himself together. Bay walked into the isle pretending he didn't see Semeya standing in the bread isle. Bay walked right up on her and bumped her shopping cart with his. "My bad." Bay turned around then looked at Semeya like he was totally surprised that he ran into her.

"Stop fronting you was there when I told Jazmine I was coming to Sam's Club."

"I don't remember that I had to pick up a few things." Bay lied.

"A few things like what?"

"Food." He frowned at Semeya.

"What kind of food?"

"Eating food the kind you eat."

"You're lying." Semeya tried to push her cart pass him. Bay put his hand out and stopped her from moving pass him.

"I aint here for no food I don't even shop here this aint even my fucking card my aunt let me use this. I got to take this shit back over there to her when I leave her. I came here because I knew you was going to be here. I came to talk to you. Why you ignoring a nigga like that?"

"You hit me."

"You serious?" The look on Bay's face made Semeya smirk then she straightened her face up.

"How do I know you're not a woman beater and you won't be beating on me whenever you get mad?"

"You dead ass right now? I'm a goon out this bitch what I look like fighting on a hoe?"

"See how you think about me a hoe you fighting on?" Semeya rolled her eyes and tried to walk pass Bay. She wasn't mad she wanted him to chase after her and give her the attention that she craved from him.

"If you wasn't who you was and meant what you mean to me I wouldn't chase behind you. I wouldn't do this I don't let females play with me like this." Bay normally didn't chase after women because most of them played games and felt like they were too good for a nigga, but be the same lonely ass bitches sitting up in the house alone at the end of the night talking about they got some good pussy that nobody trying to put a claim on. Let them tell it there isn't any good niggas worth anything around. According to Bay it wasn't that there weren't any good niggas around it was the chicks were overestimating who they were and they had these high demands with unrealistic standards then they felt like they were better than niggas besides that bitches mistake fake shit for real shit on a daily basis. They don't want to be happy they wanted to be the center of attention.

"What does that mean?"

"It means I'm not about to chase after you. If you walk away from me again I'm going to have to let you because I can't keep chasing after you without getting any positive feedback."

"Don't chase me then." Semeya walked passed Bay smiling like she was unaffected. On the inside she was piping hot burning up pissed off that he peeped what she was trying to do. Semeya walked up the isle wondering if she should slow down so that Bay could keep up with her she wondered if he was even still in the isle or if he walked away and giving up on her. It took everything in Semeya not to look over her shoulder to see if Bay was following behind her. He wasn't, but he stood perfectly still watching Semeya walk away from him. He pulled out his phone and call Jazmine.

"What happened?" Jazmine had a big kool aide smile on her face she was such a sucker for love and happy endings.

"That shit didn't work." Bay walked up the isle slowly with his head down.

"Don't give up just yet we gon' get you your girl back I'll be in touch." Jazmine hung up the phone.

"Get my girl back mother fuckers is crazy that bitch already got a man." Bay walked around for a few minutes cooling off before he walked out of front door of Sam's Club and then into the parking lot. He walked over to his car while he was unlocking his door Semeya pulled up next to him. She rolled her window down.

"Awww you look like you lost your best friend." She had a evil smile on her face.

"Why you fucking with me?" He shook his head fighting the urge to smile opened his car door. "I'm not about to kiss your ass I didn't do shit to hurt you."

"Bay." Semeya called out to him.

"What?" He looked up and into Semeya's eyes.

"Do you wanna know how I really feel?"

"How do you really feel?" Bay laughed then stuck his middle finger up. "This bitch is corny as fuck." He mumbled to himself when Semeya rolled her window up and then pulled off on him with her fingers in the air chucking up the deuces.

## Chapter 26

The next few weeks were hard on Bay he tried everything every time Semeya went anywhere Jazmine would call him and let him know where she was going to be. Like a damn fool Bay would be there waiting on her. Jazmine called him and told him that Semeya was going to the car wash so he'd better hurry up leave so he could meet her there.

Bay didn't ask any questions he got up, left the house, and got inside of his car and drove over to the car wash were Jazmine told him that Semeya would be. Bay spotted Semeya's car and parked his car he got out of his car. He walked over to the part of the car wash where Semeya would have to come out of after getting her car washed. Soon as he saw the front end of Semeya's car coming through he stood in front of her car.

"You ready to talk to me?" Bay held his arms up.

"Boy you better move your ass from in front of my car before you get ran over." Semeya pressed on the gas and then the breaks making the car jerk in his direction. "Move nigga...get your ass out of my way."

"Get out and talk to me let me explain." Bay knocked on driver's side window.

"I already heard that weak shit you was popping."

"It was real though and from my heart." Bay tried to open Semeya's car door and it was locked. "Open the door."

"Hell naw." Semeya smiled at Bay then she peeled off on him. She pulled off and burned rubber on him. Bay was feeling frustrated he had approached Semeya on seven or eight different times and she shitted on him. He was done trying that was it he wasn't doing it no more. Fuck love, all the bitches in the world, he was officially on shit. He was just gonna fuck and dog women they don't fucked around and hurt his feelings now the entire female populace was at risk of being mistreated he was on some shit. Bay pulled off with an attitude he drove around until the urge to lie down came over him. He was sadder than a eight month old baby who dropped her pacifier. Bay pulled up at his house and got out of the car he walked up to his house when he noticed someone walking from the side of his house. "What the fuck you doing back there?"

"I was going to climb in your window then I decided against it." Semeya looked at Bay with a straight face.

"Why was you going to climb through my window?"

"Why did you act like you worked for door dash, why you was at the car wash, why would at Sam's Club, Wal-mart, and everywhere else you've been popping up chasing me down all up my ass?"

"Aint nobody thinking about you." Bay mumbled under his breath.

"I saw how sad you looked when I pulled off at the car wash. I said to myself I was being a little too mean to you. I had to teach you a lesson about putting your hands on me don't ever put your hands on me."

"I'll put my hands on you right now." Bay reached out and palmed both of her breasts. Er

"You know what I mean."

"Oh like this?" Bay pulled Semeya closer into him and wrapped his arms around her back then used his other hand to grab up as much of her booty as he could fit in his hand. "You came over her for this BDE huh."

"BDE?" Semeya was lost she didn't know what he was talking about.

"This big dick energy." Bay smiled then kissed her on the lips.

"I didn't come over here for nothing like that I can't do anything no way I'm on my period."

"Shut your lying ass up." Bay squeezed her ass tighter.

"I am how you gon' tell me." Semeya lied again with a smile on her face.

"That's cool we can do it orally." Bay loved talking nasty and being mannish and that was one of the things that Semeya enjoyed about him his nasty ass mouth.

"I don't suck dick." Semeya sounded like she was half way wanted him to believe what she just said before laughing hysterically Bay had scooped her up into his arms and unlocked his front door then took her inside of the house.

"We good?" Bay looked deep into Semeya's eyes connecting with her on an internal level.

"We good." Semeya smiled and kissed Bay on the lips. "Now take me upstairs to your big bed so you can get this New York work." Semeya imitated Jazmine's voice when they were in Miami.

"I got you.

Thank you for spending time reading my book you could be doing anything else besides spending time with a little unknown writer like me.